PHONE CIPHER

KU-076-516

You need a phone keypad to crack this cipher. The code number consists of the number the letter is on the keypad, plus its position. For example, A is the 1st number on 2, so it would be 2 1.

A=21	B=22	C=23	D=31	E=32	F=33	G=41
H=42	I=43	J=51	K=52	L=53	M=61	N=62
O=63	P=71	Q=72	R=73	S=74	T=81	U=82
V=83	W=91	X=92	Y=93	Z=94		

KEYBOARD CIPHER

This cipher uses a QWERTY keyboard. To decode, just shift one letter to the right. If there isn't a letter to the right, shift in the opposite direction.

Look at a laptop or computer keyboard to help you.

FREE DOWNLOAD

Solve the ciphers and the clues as you read along! Download your free *Spy's Guide to Europe* on our website:

www.cranachanpublishing.co.uk/resources

WHERE ARE WE?

1. THIS COUNTRY'S NATIONAL ANIMAL IS A UNICORN.

2. THE NATIONAL FLAG IS KNOWN AS THE SALTIRE.

3. THIS COUNTRY HAS AROUND 790 ISLANDS.

In loving memory of Calum Wright, who
is very much missed by all his family
and friends and by his colleagues at the
Tintin shop in Brussels.

CIPHERS FOR THE EURO MÉTRO

A cipher is a system of writing that disguises the writer's message. It's like using a secret code or language to keep information safe. You will need to use the following ciphers to crack the code and discover the passwords for the Euro Métro.

CAESAR CIPHER

Julius Caesar wrote all his important correspondence in this simple alphabet cipher, which involved moving each letter three steps to the left.

A=X B=Y C=Z D=A E=B F=C G=D H=E I=F
J=G K=H L=I M=J N=K O=L P=M Q=N R=O
S=P T=Q U=R V=S W=T X=U Y=V Z=W

ATBASH CIPHER

This simple cipher, originally used for the Hebrew alphabet, is just the alphabet backwards.

A=Z B=Y C=X D=W E=V F=U G=T H=S I=R
J=Q K=P L=O M=N N=M O=L P=K Q=J R=I
S=H T=G U=F V=E W=D X=C Y=B Z=A

AN UNEXPECTED MÉTRO

Samia Chaudry had always believed that the Glasgow underground system was small and circular, so it was a shock to discover that they were travelling to Paris by Métro.

When Samia gave her mum and dad a goodbye hug at Central Station, she and her parents presumed the black cab was heading for the airport. Samia was looking forward to the flight and was fizzing with excitement when she leapt into the taxi's back seat.

'Hi, guys!' She smiled at the boy and girl squeezed in beside her, recognising them both from their newspaper photos. 'Isn't this amazing? I've never even been on a plane before! Well, apparently my parents took me to Malaga when I was three, but I can't remember anything about it, even though Mum says I was an actual nightmare and screamed for three and a half hours without stopping, cos they'd left my favourite teddy in the house and—'

Miss Watson turned from the front passenger seat and interrupted Samia's story, her voice curt. 'We're not flying. Not on this leg of the trip at least.'

When Miss Watson explained what was *actually* happening, doubts started to squirm in Samia's stomach, and Frankie didn't appear convinced either.

'Och, Miss. That's a load o mince.' Frankie looked small for his age, which was twelve according to the article in the Daily Record, but he seemed to have no fear of authority figures. 'You can't get any further south than Govan on the subway. You've as much chance of reaching Mars as France.'

Miss Watson smiled, in a rather condescending manner. 'Well, Francis. Let's see, shall we?'

When she sat back, Frankie rolled his eyes and hissed at Samia. 'Might have known this was too guid to be true. We're bein scammed.'

Two minutes later, the taxi driver stopped the cab in Argyll Street. Samia looked across at St Enoch's subway station and wondered if Frankie was right.

This was the best prize she'd ever won, better even than the History Hero certificate she'd won at primary school. She had been so excited about the prospect of a trip to Europe. Maybe too excited to think clearly. Had she and the other two kids been tricked? Was this some kind of extended prank? Were they going to be made fools of on Saturday night telly? But it couldn't be a trick—it had to be real...

Miss Watson was already out of the cab. She flung open the back door, impatience furrowing her brow.

'Come along, children. We need to make haste. Wake up, girl, for heaven's sake.'

She leaned in and shook Ava's shoulder. Ava, who had been slumped, eyes closed, against the back seat, yawned and stretched like a cat. She'd barely said a word so far, and Samia, who'd been hoping to make friends on this trip, wasn't too impressed.

She goes to a posh school in Edinburgh. Bet she's a snob and Frankie and me aren't rich enough for her...

As the three children followed Miss Watson across the busy street, Samia reflected that Ava, with her hunched shoulders and bored expression, couldn't look less thrilled about the prospect of visiting Europe.

In total contrast, Samia could feel bubbles of joy popping in her stomach, although that might have been hunger, since she hadn't eaten since lunch and it was almost seven o'clock in the evening, well past her usual dinner time.

When they arrived in the subway station, Miss Watson paused.

'Oh, heavens. I forgot to check the current Euro Métro password.' She tapped on her phone. 'The code letters are QFQXKFZ. Ava, can you assist?'

Ava yawned, but she took the phone, rolled her eyes and handed it back to Miss Wilson.

'Seriously? A basic Caesar Cipher?' The girl's voice dripped with disdain. 'You don't need hackers for that stuff. A kid who knows the alphabet could solve this code in seconds.'

'Both the code type and password are changed every couple of days. But you're right. Security needs to be tightened. Especially after what's happened.' Miss Watson beckoned at Ava. 'Since you've worked out the password, you can come with me to buy the tickets.'

As they walked away, Samia turned to Frankie, feeling baffled. 'I've heard of a Caesar Salad, but what the heck's a Caesar Cipher?'

Frankie shrugged. 'They both sound mingin. McDonald's chicken nuggets, all the way.'

Samia watched Miss Watson march over to the ticket booth, the heels of her smart black patent shoes clicking on the tiles. Samia guessed the woman was in her thirties, although it was hard to tell. She was wearing a beautiful vintage blue velvet coat with a fake-fur collar, and with her crimped hair and old-fashioned shoes she wouldn't have looked out of place on a World War 2 film set. Frankie was clearly watching her too, because she heard him muttering.

'Miss Watson talks posh, an that's why nobody asked any questions, but something weird's going on here.'

Samia bit her lip, but the worry didn't have time to form, because Miss Watson was heading back towards them, waving orange tickets, a bright smile painted on her face.

'Our train leaves in five minutes. Let the journey commence! Travelling to six—or maybe seven—countries in as many days is no small feat, so I hope you all have bags of energy!'

Sighing, as if this was all deeply dull, Ava followed Miss Watson on to the escalator, but Samia held back, waiting for Frankie to finish tying the laces of his trainers.

So, is it six or seven? Why's she being vague? Surely she knows. Hasn't this trip been planned for ages? Still, at least six countries! Wow!!

The prospect was so amazing, Samia felt she could have cartwheeled down the escalator, though she appreciated it would be a risky manoeuvre, so restrained herself.

Frankie straightened up and she grinned at him, but he was still looking doubtful.

'Reckon it *is* a scam? I mean… do you think that wummin's up to no good?' He scratched his shaven head, eyes narrowed in suspicion. 'Maybe she's plannin to chop us up an feed our deid bodies to the sharks.'

It was as if he'd thrown cold water over Samia's head. She took a step back from the escalator.

Should I go and find a phone and call Mum and Dad? Tell them the travel arrangements seem a bit peculiar? But, if I put any doubts in my parents' minds, it's all over. They'll come running—take me straight home. This trip won't happen.

Shrugging, she tried to make a joke of it. 'The

chopping up part seems unlikely. There are no sharks in the Clyde, and I doubt there are any in the river Seine.'

A businessman, in a hurry to catch his train home, pushed past, and headed down the escalator. Steadying herself, Samia made up her mind. 'Do you know what, Frankie? I really, REALLY want to go to Europe, so I'm going to risk it.'

Picking up her rucksack, she stepped on to the escalator, and when she turned to check, Frankie was right behind her.

But all the way down, she wondered if she was doing the right thing.

Miss Watson had been *very* convincing when she turned up at St Saviour's High and announced that Samia had won first prize in the Scottish School's European Culture Competition. And Samia's parents had been besides themselves with pride when her photograph had been in the *Ayrshire Post*.

First Year Pupil Wins Top Prize of A Whirlwind Tour of Europe!

Underneath, in much smaller print, the article had explained that two other first years from different parts of Scotland had won the same prize: Frankie McVicar from Carntyne in Glasgow and Ava Hamilton from Bruntsfield in Edinburgh. It also explained that the competition, organised by a recently registered charity, *European Culture For Schools*, had required a 500-word essay on why the pupil wanted to visit Europe. Nobody, either at school or at home had questioned any of it, but now, the unlikely travel arrangements and Miss Watson's vague remark about *six—or maybe seven—countries* were causing doubts to creep like spiders into Samia's brain.

Is Frankie right? Is it some kind of scam? Or worse?

They reached the bottom of the escalator where Ava was slumped against the tiled wall, eyes half-closed. In total contrast, Miss Watson's foot was tapping, her face taut.

'Get a move on you two, for goodness' sake. We mustn't miss the train. It's a weekly service, don't you know, and restricted to very important people!'

'Aye, in your dreams,' muttered Frankie.

'I am deadly serious, Francis. This service is for government officials, high-ranking civil servants and European delegates. It is a real privilege to be granted permission to use these trains and we must make the most of the opportunity.'

Veering to the left, Miss Watson waved her tickets under the nose of a weary looking guard, and led the way down a narrow, dimly-lit corridor. On the brick tiled floors, Ava's suitcase wheels rattled like hail on windows.

The passageway opened out onto a narrow, empty platform. The only signage was a rectangular metal plaque on the wall.

Glasgow City

Miss Watson spoke in a bossy tone that was already grating on Samia's nerves.

'Stand back, children. The train's coming.'

Her hearing must have been sharp, because it was only when she ushered them back from the platform's edge, that Samia heard the echoey, whooshing rumble of an arriving underground train and saw the eerie glow of its headlights.

With a screech of brakes, the train slowed to a stop, right in front of them. Frankie swore in appreciation.

Even Ava sounded impressed. 'Wow. Classy paintwork.'

Samia nodded. 'It's gorgeous.'

This train was nothing like the bog-standard Glasgow underground version. Its shape was torpedo-like, sleek and smooth. Its livery was gorgeous; Morpho-butterfly-blue with a gleaming silver stripe. There were two carriages, both with darkened windows, but only the back carriage's doors slid open.

Samia hoisted her rucksack, and stepped on board first, doubts crushed, excitement zinging.

It's actually happening! We're going to freaking Paris!

2

A CRYPTIC MESSAGE

Holding on to a polished rail, Samia stood and admired the carriage's interior as the others boarded behind her.

Excellent... Comfy seating... soft blue velvety material... shiny floor... fancy swivelly tables... this is smarter than your average subway carriage... it even smells yummy, as if someone's lit a vanilla candle.

Frankie whistled. 'No bad, eh?'

'Fact.' Samia smiled. 'And check the sign—there's free wi-fi and phone charging points! Oh...'

She groaned, and Frankie gave a deep, heartfelt sigh. 'I already miss my phone more than I miss my maw.'

Miss Watson finished stowing her suitcase in a rack and gave Frankie a hard stare.

'I do hope you've stuck to the rules, Francis, because I *will* confiscate any electronic gadgets.'

'Aye, it said in the email, an I can read fine, but why? It doesn't make any sense.'

'Frankie's right.' Samia gulped, as Miss Watson's chilly expression fixed on her, but she kept speaking, as she was so convinced she was right, and that the no-phone-rule was unjust and unreasonable. 'It doesn't make sense. We could have taken lots of photos with the cameras on our phones and surely your charity would have benefited from all the social media attention?'

Miss Watson took off her lovely coat, sat down and rummaged in her copious handbag. She drew out three small foil-wrapped packages.

'Our charity's insurance policy doesn't cover expensive electronics for minors. But we are kindly providing you with a perfectly acceptable alternative— these cheap and cheerful disposable cameras. Take all the photographs you wish.' She handed the cameras over, the stern expression still on her face. 'The charity shall be responsible for any social media posts. I expect they will do a lovely article about our adventure once it is at an end.'

Frankie stared at the package in disbelief, and Ava didn't even attempt to disguise her sneer, as she threw herself down and stuffed the camera in the pocket of her leather jacket. 'Well, there's a throwback to the last millennium.'

'I'll sit across here, so I can stretch my legs.' Frankie waved towards a seat at the other side of the carriage, but Miss Watson shook her head.

'You'll do no such thing. We shall sit here, together at this table.'

Frankie looked up and down the aisle.

'Eh, why? There's loads o room to spread out.'

Miss Watson clicked her tongue. 'Francis, you signed the contract. One of its terms is that you will follow my instructions. And I have just given one, which you are failing to follow. Do you wish to return home now? Because it can be arranged. The train hasn't yet left the station.'

Scowling, Frankie slid into the seat next to Samia.

'Are there any other stops?' Samia asked, wondering if perhaps the carriage was about to get busier. 'Between here and Paris, I mean?'

'There may be.'

It was such an annoyingly cryptic reply that Samia was about to ask Miss Watson to clarify, but before she could speak there was a loud warning bleep, and an electronic announcement.

'This train is ready to leave. Please mind the doors. Next station, Paris... or possibly London.'

Samia shook her head in disbelief. 'I've never been on a train that wasn't sure where it was stopping.'

The carriage doors slid shut.

As the train began to move, shoogling through the tunnels, steadily building up speed, Samia exhaled, a long breath that misted the window.

We're on our way! Paris—or maybe London—here I come!

She hugged herself, and smiled at Ava, who blinked,

as if unsure how to respond. To Samia's annoyance, she then resumed her disinterested expression and started picking at the chipped nail varnish on her fingernails, gazing out the window at her own reflection, as the train travelled through the darkness.

Samia settled back in her seat.

Well, Ava's not exactly a laugh a minute. I can't understand why the heck she entered the competition, when she clearly thinks being a prize winner is a pain in the butt. I can picture it now, me and Frankie clicking away with our disposable cameras, while Ava trails behind, moaning her face off. But at least I'm going to see Europe. And I'm going to have a wonderful time, even if Miss Watson keeps carping about 'the rules' non-stop. When we reach Paris, I'll buy earplugs.

She gazed at Miss Watson, wondering about her motivation for leading this expedition, when she clearly had no time for children. The woman's head was bent, but her bobbed hair, black as a raven's wing and rippled like silk, stayed neatly in place. She was studying a small scrap of paper, and Samia wondered what she was reading so intently, and why it was causing her forehead to furrow and her lips to purse as if she'd tasted something sour. Remembering that she'd packed her favourite travel book, *Famous European Landmarks*, Samia pulled it out of the rucksack at her feet and started leafing through it, while beside her, Frankie dived into his own bag and pulled out a packet of pickled onion Monster Munch and a bottle of Coke.

Miss Watson looked up from her paper. 'Put those away, Francis. We will be dining shortly.'

Frankie's eyes narrowed. 'Aye, but how long's shortly? I'm starvin the now.'

He took a rebellious swig of his Coke, but put the crisps back in his bag.

Samia felt her stomach rumble and wished she'd forward planned like Frankie and brought along some snacks.

How long WAS shortly? she wondered. *And how long will this part of the journey take? Will we have to sleep on these seats?*

She was about to ask aloud, when Miss Watson spoke. 'Samia, may I have a quick look at your book?'

Samia glanced up and noticed a calculating expression in the woman's eyes that belied her casual tone.

'Sure. I've read this book so many times! I'm sure it's the reason I won the prize, cos I've learned so much from it about European history and art. It's—'

Again, Miss Watson interrupted her attempt to chat. 'Just let me look for myself, please.'

Feeling a little flicker of annoyance, Samia slid the book across the table. Miss Watson's crimson painted nails drummed on the cover, before she lifted it and flicked to a well-thumbed page. She stared at the *Paris*

Landmarks double page spread, crammed with facts about the Eiffel Tower, Montmartre, and the Louvre.

Her head snapped up, and her eyes fixed on Samia, with the same calculating expression.

'You're keen on art, aren't you? Tell me what you know about the Louvre.'

Samia reeled off a few facts, mostly borrowed from her guidebook.

'It's the largest art museum in the world, and the most visited. Its most famous painting is the Mona Lisa by Leonardo da Vinci.'

'Do you know anything about the other art works in the museum?'

'Well, I've googled. I've checked out the different galleries. The one I'm super keen to visit has—'

Miss Watson cut her off, waving the piece of flimsy blue paper under the girl's nose.

'Do you recognise a painting from this... um... description? No worries if not; it's just a puzzle I'm doing with a... colleague.' She smiled, a tight, anxious smile, that curved her lips but didn't warm her face or light her eyes. 'Just a little game.'

Frankie leant forward. 'Let's see.'

He snatched the paper from Samia's fingers, read it quickly and then flicked it back across the table.

'Your "game" makes no sense, hen.'

Before Ava could grab the note too, not that she was

showing the slightest bit of interest, Samia picked it up. The pencilled writing was a messy scrawl, words flying over the paper as if whoever had written them had been in a massive rush.

Small planet putting on his shoes

She cocked her head, trying to work out what the note meant.

It wasn't a description of any painting she'd ever heard of, that was for sure.

Shrugging, Samia passed the paper back to Miss Watson. 'Frankie's right. It doesn't make sense.'

Miss Watson placed the paper inside her old-fashioned handbag and snapped the clasp shut, just as the door to the other carriage slid open. 'Ah, here comes Gabrielle. Excellent timing.'

Gabrielle was a tall, stick-thin middle-aged lady, with cropped, greying hair. She was dressed in chef's whites and pushing a trolley, topped with four plates covered with silver domes. She stopped in front of their table, and without saying a word, began setting it with linen place mats and silver cutlery.

Then with a splendid flourish, she placed a plate in front of each person, and lifted the domes one by one. Ava had a massive juicy burger and hand-cut chips, Frankie's meal was a gigantic mound of spaghetti carbonara, Miss Watson had teriyaki salmon with noodles, and Samia had a pepperoni pizza; her all-time favourite meal.

Frankie poked his fork into his pasta, suspicion in his eyes. 'How did you lot know spaghetti carbonara's my favourite?'

Gabrielle passed him a napkin and didn't reply.

'Those details were on the form you all filled in last week,' said Miss Watson. 'Remember? Favourite meal, favourite movie etc, etc. The questions weren't asked for no reason. Francis, what sort of way is that to eat spaghetti, for heaven's sake!'

Unruffled, Frankie gave her a hard stare. 'The right way.'

Samia picked up a slice of pizza, and bit into it, wondering if Miss Watson would start criticising her methods too.

Gabrielle didn't move away. She waited by the trolley, arms folded, her eyes fixed on Miss Watson. And then she spoke for the first time, and to Samia's surprise, her voice was choked with fury.

'It isn't right! They're little children!' Gabrielle was almost spitting with rage. 'You've no right to endanger them like this!'

She tossed her head, so the chef's hat slipped over her eyes, and when she started to wheel the trolley backwards, it knocked against a table, sending a silver dome clattering to the floor.

Miss Watson's mouth had been round with shock, but she collected herself quickly.

'Just bring us our desserts, Gabrielle, please. And

keep your foolish opinions to yourself.'

Frankie slurped up another strand of spaghetti. 'What's she on about? What does she mean we're *endangered*? We're not rhinos.'

Ava picked up a chip, dipped it in ketchup and wagged it at Miss Watson like a blood-splattered finger. 'Bang, bang. We're dead.'

Samia gulped. 'What's going on?'

Miss Watson had gone very pale, but her mouth was set in a firm line.

'There were a few, minor, unimportant details I omitted from the trip letter and I shall explain those at breakfast tomorrow. We shall eat our desserts, have a good night's sleep, and will arrive in Paris fresh as daisies. There is nothing, I repeat, nothing at all, for you children to worry about. All will be well, you'll see.'

Samia felt the sharp jut of an elbow in her ribs. She gave Frankie a sideways glance and saw he'd formed a word from the last strands of spaghetti on his nearly empty plate.

LIAR

WHERE ARE WE?

1. THIS COUNTRY WAS ONCE RULED BY TUDOR KINGS AND QUEENS.

2. THE PATRON SAINT IS ST GEORGE.

3. ITS LARGEST LAKE IS LAKE WINDERMERE.

A SHOT IN THE DARK

Gabrielle returned, stony-faced and silent, pushing a dessert trolley laden with raspberry cheesecake, trifle, and a chocolate mountain of profiteroles. Samia tucked into her massive slice of cheesecake, savouring every delicious, creamy mouthful. Her enjoyment of the food was making it hard to think, but she was keen to try and work out what on earth was going on.

*This is getting weirder by the moment. Gabrielle said Miss Watson had no right to put us in danger. Miss Watson said there was nothing for us children to worry about. Does that mean **she's** worrying? Is she in some kind of danger?*

And does it have something to do with the message on that scrap of paper?

Fastidiously, Miss Watson dabbed at the corner of her mouth with a linen napkin.

'I think an early night is definitely in order. Be up for breakfast at seven on the dot. We should arrive in central Paris by eight and I have a busy day of excursions planned.' She paused. 'If the train stops during the night, stay in your rooms and keep your doors locked. That is an order.'

Frankie laughed. 'Eh? What rooms? This is a tarted-up subway carriage, no a B&B.'

Miss Watson laid the napkin on the table. 'Gabrielle, show the children to their cabins please. And then bring me a black coffee.'

Gabrielle murmured something unintelligible under her breath.

The three children left their seats and followed her towards the front carriage. When the doors to the front carriage slid open, they entered a narrow, wood-panelled passageway.

'Toilets and showers are at the end of this corridor, on the right.'

When Gabrielle pressed a button, one of the panels shot open, revealing a tiny cabin with bunkbeds and a miniature sink.

She nodded at Frankie. 'This is your room.'

'Just for me, I hope. I'm no sharin wi lassies or that scary wummin.'

'You've got it all to yourself. Now, get inside and lock the door. Whatever happens in the night, don't open it.'

'As if.' Frankie grinned and hopped inside his cabin. 'I'm no as daft as I look.'

Casually, as if she hadn't just given a chilling warning, Gabrielle punched another button and gestured at Ava and Samia. 'You two *are* sharing.'

Unexpectedly, she put her hand on Samia's shoulder. 'I am so sorry you've been dragged into this dangerous *situation*. It's outrageous...'

Rudely, Ava pushed past them. 'Bagsy the bottom bunk.' Throwing her wheeled suitcase onto the blue and silver striped duvet, she plonked herself down beside it.

Samia didn't move. 'What exactly is going on?' she asked Gabrielle. 'Why did you say Miss Watson has put us in danger?'

But Gabrielle wasn't looking at Samia. Her gaze was fixed on Ava, who was staring up at her, eyes flint-hard, as if daring her to speak.

Gabrielle laughed nervously. 'It was a little joke! Of course, there is no danger! It is only common sense to keep the cabin door locked, as we may stop in London, and more passengers might embark. Now, in you get. Have a restful sleep. The mattresses are sprung, and the duvets are hypoallergenic. All will be well.'

But Gabrielle's fingers had tightened their grip on Samia's shoulder, so hard her nails dug into her skin, and Samia sensed she didn't believe for a moment that all would be well.

Once the two girls were alone, Samia's curiosity finally got the better of her.

'So, what was the Euro Métro password?'

When Ava told her, she shivered, and glanced out

the window, at the pitch-black tunnel. 'Hope *we're* not hurtling through the darkness towards our doom.'

Ava shrugged, and pulled a pair of pjs out of her bag. 'There's every chance we're doing exactly that. So, we'd better get some sleep in the meantime.'

Samia blinked at her companion. She had to be joking, *surely*. But Ava's face was unsmiling.

Despite her misgivings, Samia *was* tired, and sleep seemed the only sensible activity. Once she'd washed, she clambered up the metal steps and found a narrow but comfortable bed. There was a little reading light and two soft pillows. It was all very cosy, and as long as Ava didn't snore, she imagined she'd be able to sleep very well.

And she did, for quite a while. It must have been the early hours of the morning when she was woken by the screech of brakes and a loud whistle.

In the bottom bunk, Ava stirred.

Samia leaned over and whispered. 'Do you think we're in London?'

There was no reply.

Don't pretend to be asleep. I know you're awake too.

'We have arrived at London Euston. Mind the gap when exiting this train.'

Samia lay, wakeful, listening to doors swishing open, a murmur of voices as people got on the train.

'This train is ready to leave. Please stand back from the doors. Next station, Paris Gare de Lyon.'

Everything's okay. It's just more passengers getting on board. No big deal.

As the train started to move again, a buzz of anticipation zapped through Samia's body.

We'll be going under the sea soon. Heading for France.

She wriggled under the covers, hoping to get back to sleep for a few more hours.

And then there was a bang on the cabin door.

Heart thudding in her chest, Samia sat up in bed, and clicked on her reading light, just as Ava leapt from her bunk and moved towards the door. Panicking, Samia squealed. 'Miss Watson said we weren't to open it!'

Ava turned, giving her a withering look. 'Do I look stupid?'

There was another rap on the door. 'Tickets please!' called a male voice. There was a pause. '*Vos billets, s'il vous plaît!*'

Ava scowled, her eyes glinting in the half-light. Her back was bent against the door as if she was trying to physically prevent the stranger from entering the cabin.

'Do you think it might be an actual ticket collector?' asked Samia. It didn't seem outwith the realms of possibility. After all, they were on a train.

Ava shook her head so hard that strands of her bright magenta hair swung like pink streamers.

'Course not. Rail staff don't disturb passengers in the middle of the night.'

Don't they? Who the heck is it then?

Samia's stomach tightened. She pulled the covers up further, wondering if she should hide. Behind the door, the man spoke again, his voice gruff, accent indiscernible.

'I need to see your tickets. Open the door. *Ouvrez la porte.*'

'He doesn't know if we speak French or English, so he doesn't know who's in here. He's just fishing.' Ava was speaking so quietly that Samia wasn't sure if she was talking to her or reassuring herself.

Outside the cabin, someone else spoke—a female voice, sharp with annoyance.

'What are you doing here? That cabin's occupied. Go back to your seat.'

Samia recognised the voice. 'Gabrielle…'

Fear flickered in Ava's eyes. 'Oh no. I hope she doesn't do anything stu—'

Crash!

Samia jumped so hard, she almost fell out of the bed.

The crash was followed by a series of dull, rhythmic thuds, as if a boxer was pounding a punchbag.

When Samia heard a muffled groan, her stomach tightened with anxiety.

Clinging to the bunk side as if she were on a life raft, her heartbeat racing, Samia whimpered. 'What's going on out there?'

'*Shh!* How am I meant to find out when you're whinging at me?'

Ava's ear was against the door, her face set like stone.

Resisting the urge to pull the duvet over her head and hide, Samia swung down from the top bunk and hurried over to join her.

When she pressed her ear to the door, Samia heard a horrible choking sound, as if someone was struggling for breath.

'Do you think he's trying to strangle Gabrielle?'

'Shut up, will you?'

Samia heard the tremble in Ava's voice, and realised the girl was really scared.

Fear churning in her stomach, Samia did as she was told and stayed silent.

The choking sounds stopped. A sudden sharp crack, like a bone breaking, shattered the quiet. The heavy, ominous thump that followed chilled Samia's blood.

Ava's hand flew to her mouth. 'Someone's been shot.'

Samia gulped, sick with horror. '*What*? Did you say shot?'

'*Shh!*'

They stayed by the door, statue-still, listening, but there was silence outside, apart from a distant rattle and the rhythmic rumbling of the train.

Ava's shoulders sagged. In the glow of the reading light, Samia saw a glimmer of relief in her eyes.

'Scary moment,' she breathed. 'But Gabrielle's clearly not to be messed with.'

Samia wrapped her arms round her body, trying to stop herself from shaking.

'How do you know *he* hasn't killed *her*?'

Ava sighed, as if Samia had said something impossibly stupid.

'Did you hear that rattling sound? That's the noise Gabrielle's trolley makes. Bet she's wheeling that guy's corpse to the luggage compartment right now.' She paused. 'And also, if that guy had just shot Gabrielle, he'd have taken her master key, got in this room and would be asking lots of questions of *us* right now. And then we'd be the ones with the gun pointing at us. We've literally just dodged a bullet. Well, two bullets, technically—or more if he's a lousy shot.'

Samia slumped onto the bottom bunk, hugging herself in an attempt to stop the trembling in her body. 'But why would anyone want to hurt us? We're only kids. We're not a threat to anyone. What's going on, Ava?'

She glared at Ava, and Ava glared back, until the tension made the tiny room feel claustrophobic. Ava blinked first, and for a moment, Samia thought she might be about to open up, but then she gave one of her maddening shrugs and sauntered over to the bunk.

'I don't know any more than you, do I? I'm on a tedious school trip to Europe. Same as you. Bet the booby prize was two trips.' She yawned widely, showing a mouthful of perfect teeth.

'Anyway, Miss Watson said she'll tell us more in the morning. And I'm shattered, and would quite like to go back to sleep, so bog off, will you?'

Samia didn't move. She fixed Ava with another accusing stare. 'You knew that guy had been shot, just by the sound. How did you know that?'

Ava rolled her eyes. 'Jeez. Do you not watch crime dramas on the telly? Everyone knows that stuff. Come on, Samia. I need some sleep and so do you. Promise, I know nothing.'

She crawled past and tugged at the duvet.

With a deep sigh, Samia stood up and climbed the steps to the top bunk.

She's lying, I'm sure of it. She knows more than she's letting on. And all that "I'm so bored" stuff is just an act.

Throwing herself down on the bed, Samia snuggled under the covers, enjoying the duvet's cosy warmth. She imagined getting back to sleep would be impossible for them both, but Ava seemed to drop off right away, if her slow, steady breathing was anything to go by. And after a few minutes of staring at the ceiling, worries flitting like bats, Samia felt herself drifting off, brain soothed by the clattering, rolling rhythm of the train.

WHERE ARE WE?

1. THIS COUNTRY IS THE LARGEST IN WESTERN EUROPE.

2. ITS FLAG IS KNOWN AS THE TRICOLORE.

3. THIS COUNTRY HAD A MONARCHY UNTIL THE REVOLUTION IN 1789.

4

STRANGER ON A BRIDGE

When Samia and Ava entered the dining carriage the next morning, Miss Watson was sitting at their usual table, speaking in an undertone to Gabrielle, who was poised by the breakfast trolley, sharp-eyed as a heron in a pond.

'Good morning, girls. I trust you slept well.'

Samia blinked. *Surely Miss Watson must have heard the noises in the hallway last night?*

She looked closely at Gabrielle. Her chef's whites were pristine and she was wearing a jaunty checked neckerchief.

She wasn't wearing that last night. Is she trying to cover bruising on her throat?

'Good morning. Miss Watson. Gabrielle, are you okay? We heard—'

Miss Watson waved an imperious hand, then picked up a slice of toast and started smearing it with butter.

'Samia, please stop chattering. Sit down and eat your breakfast, which should be exactly as requested.'

As usual, Miss Watson looked intimidatingly smart,

in an emerald green linen dress and pearl-buttoned cardigan, her hair and make-up immaculate.

Samia did as she was told. Ava plonked herself down beside Miss Watson, and licked her lips when Gabrielle put a stack of fluffy pancakes in front of her, and a little jug of glistening maple syrup.

As Gabrielle silently placed her dish of scrambled eggs and bacon on the table, Samia heard the connecting door swish open. She looked up and saw Frankie sauntering down the aisle, his cropped hair gelled in tiny hedgehog spikes. But it was his expression that really caught her attention. Frowning, eyes narrowed—he looked really annoyed.

Flinging himself down next to Samia, he growled at Miss Watson.

'What the heck was aw that about? Someone was bangin on my door, sayin they wanted to see my ticket, in the middle of the soddin night! An then they started a freakin rammy outside my cabin! Is this the bloomin party train, or what?'

'Calm down, dear.' Miss Watson smoothed a linen napkin across her knees. 'Gabrielle has just informed me that several passengers boarded in London, and one or two had over-imbibed. Those gentlemen will be sleeping off their hangovers this morning, I expect.'

Samia glanced at Ava and caught her rolling her eyes. She waited until Gabrielle had served Frankie's

30

breakfast—two rolls and square sausage slathered in brown sauce—and had trundled off with her trolley.

'Yesterday, you said…' Samia waggled her fork at Miss Watson, trying to recall the woman's exact words. 'You said there were a few details you'd neglected to mention about this trip and you'd tell us more this morning. Something about it being dangerous?'

'Aye.' Frankie bit into his roll. 'Gabrielle said we're only weans an you've no right to endanger us. Or words to that effect.'

Miss Watson wiped the corner of her mouth with her napkin and poured herself more tea.

She seemed to be avoiding their gaze.

'Actually, there is nothing to tell. I had a small concern about the… um… travel arrangements, but that worry has been… er… *eliminated*. So, let us finish our breakfast in peace and then we can get organised and collect our luggage. In twenty minutes or so, *on arrive à Paris!*'

Samia crunched on her toast, her thoughts whirling.

A concern has been eliminated. Is she talking about the man who was shot?

One thing was for sure. No further facts were going to be forthcoming. Miss Watson's eyes were steely, her expression firm. And Ava seemed more interested in tackling her massive stack of pancakes than interrogating Miss Watson.

A balding, bearded man was sitting alone at the end

of the carriage, sipping coffee and chewing on a bagel, totally engrossed in his newspaper.

Who was he? These trains were for VIPs, Miss Watson had said, and the carriages were so fancy, she could well believe it. Was that man some kind of government official maybe? A diplomat or foreign ambassador? As Samia attempted to spy on him, without drawing attention to herself, an elderly lady shuffled past and sat at the table opposite. She was swathed in a purple tartan cape and her short curly hair was dyed violet, which toned rather nicely with her outfit.

She caught Samia's eye and smiled.

'Is this your first trip to Paris, my dear?'

Her voice was soft, her accent English. She sounded utterly harmless, but before Samia could reply, Miss Watson stood up, and clicked her heels, like Dorothy in Oz.

'Come now, children! Hurry along. Francis, wipe your chin, please.'

Frankie rubbed at his sauce-smeared chin, and Miss Watson groaned despairingly. 'I meant with the napkin, child. Not your sleeve.'

The elderly lady was still smiling, but something about her was starting to trouble Samia. Behind her spectacles, her eyes were sharp, her expression cunning. Her hands were covered by her cape.

Ava said the train security systems are too easy to hack. Maybe that woman's up to no good. What if she's in league with the guy from last night? Perhaps she's hiding a weapon. Or maybe I'm getting paranoid... suspecting innocent old ladies of being armed assassins.

Deciding it wasn't wise to speak to strangers at the best of times, Samia looked away and let Miss Watson usher her from the carriage and back to their rooms, without even attempting to answer the old lady's question.

Twenty minutes later, the brakes screeched as the train drew into the Gare De Lyon station.

'This is an extremely busy station, so stay close!' ordered Miss Watson as they stepped off the train. 'If you get lost, it will be on your own heads.'

Behind Miss Watson's back, Ava stuck out her tongue.

'On *our* heads? Don't think so,' she muttered. 'She's the one who'll be held responsible. *She's* meant to be in charge.'

All the same, Samia did her best to keep up with Miss Watson. Being lost in this milling crowd was not an appealing prospect. As they headed up the stairs towards street level, and dropped off their luggage in the lockers, her pulse quickened. Caught in the crowds surging out of the exit, she scrambled to catch up with the others, and joined them on the pavement.

Blinking in the sunlight, Samia gazed around at the tall, elegant buildings with their wrought iron balconies, the shops with their colourful awnings, the cafés with their crowded outside tables. The city buzzed with movement and noise: beeping car horns, wailing sirens, loud chatter from the commuters streaming from the métro.

Miss Watson pointed to the station's chic green sign.

'Métro is short for metropolitan—the word means *of a city*. But it also refers to the characteristics of a city's inhabitants: cultured, sophisticated, accepting of new people and new ideas. I fully expect you three to be metropolitans by the time this trip is over!'

She beamed at them, and patted Frankie's spiky hair. 'Of course, Francis has a head start on the rest of us, being fluent in French, Italian and German.'

Samia gasped, genuinely impressed. 'Wow, Frankie. That's amazing.'

Frankie didn't seem to know how to react to praise. He scowled and turned away. Then his face brightened. 'Excellent. There's a McDonald's. *S'il vous plaît, est-ce que je peux avoir un cheeseburger?*'

Miss Watson sighed and checked her watch.

'Certainly not. You've just had breakfast. Let us begin our tour!'

The children scuttled behind Miss Watson as she marched, first pointing out the site of the Bastille, the old prison destroyed during the revolution.

Frankie was less than impressed. 'It's just a flamin roundabout. You'd think they'd have left some severed heids for the tourists.'

They took a short detour to check out the colourful houseboats moored on the banks of the Bassin de l'Arsenal.

'I'd love to live on a houseboat,' said Ava, her voice wistful. 'Just me and my cat.'

'What's your cat's name?' asked Samia, pleased to discover they'd one thing in common, at least. 'Mine is called Dave, cos we thought she was a boy-cat. She likes to catch—'

Ava cut her off. 'I don't have a cat. It was a wish. Not real-life.'

They stopped briefly at a café in Le Marais to sit in the sunshine and drink Cokes, while Miss Watson sipped on a black coffee, before continuing over the Pont d'Arcole and onwards, only slowing briefly to view the fire-damaged cathedral at Notre Dame.

Halfway across the Pont Neuf, Miss Watson stopped, and began a mini-history lesson entitled, The Oldest Bridge in Paris. Samia, who was glad of the brief rest, as her feet were beginning to hurt, looked at her companions and wondered if Miss Watson realised she was in danger of losing her audience. Ava was reading the messages on the profusion of padlocks attached to the railings and Frankie was leaning over the wall so far he was in danger of falling in the water.

'Ironically, although its name translates as New Bridge, this is the oldest bridge spanning the Seine in the city.'

Miss Watson paused, to take a breath. 'Interestingly...'

Even for a history geek, bridges weren't that interesting. Samia switched off. The sun was warm on her back as she looked down at the river below. The open excursion boats were full of tourists, and she envied them their relaxing tours, seeing the sights without having to walk around in this heat.

But when she looked to the left, a chill snaked up her spine.

An elderly woman was heading towards them, dressed too warmly for the weather in a garish tartan cape.

It's the old lady from the train. She's following us.

'Oi, Samia!' called Frankie. 'I'm goin to take your picture. Smile!'

Smiling, Samia spun round. When she turned back, the old lady had vanished.

'Right, children! Time to move along!'

Miss Watson ushered them onwards, towards the Louvre.

But when Samia glanced round, the woman from the train had reappeared, heading slowly but steadily towards them, her left hand tucked within her cape.

5

A PUZZLE TO BE SOLVED

As they entered the museum through the magnificent Louvre Pyramid, its hundreds of lozenge-shaped and triangular glass panels sparkled like jewels in the sunlight.

The sight had a startling effect on Ava. Her shoulders straightened, and her expression changed, from half-asleep to totally alert. In contrast, Miss Watson seemed to have lost some of the energy that had been propelling them around Paris. When she'd purchased their tickets, she stood looking around, her forehead furrowed, as if she'd no idea where to start.

The old woman wasn't in the ticket queue. But the place was huge, and it would be easy to stay out of view. Drawing closer to Frankie, Samia whispered in his ear.

'Last night, on the train… the fight you heard. There was a guy trying to get into our room, and Ava thinks Gabrielle shot him dead. And the old lady who was in the carriage this morning… she's following us now, though I don't know if Miss Watson has spotted her. You were right. There's something *really* strange going on.'

For a moment she was worried Frankie would think she was joking and laugh, but his eyes widened, and he stood very still, weighing the evidence.

'I knew there was somethin off about aw this.' He nudged her. 'Bet you a grand it's got somethin to do with that note.'

As well as the tickets, Miss Watson was clutching a familiar scrap of blue paper. Screwing up her face, Samia tried to remember exactly what was written on it.

'Oh yes, the cryptic message: *Small planet putting on his shoes.*'

In the vast, echoing space of the Louvre's entrance foyer, her voice carried.

Both Ava and Miss Watson's heads snapped round, and they stared at Samia. An unsettling truth dawned in Samia's brain.

Both of them know stuff about this trip that me and Frankie don't.

'Hush,' Miss Watson hissed. 'Walls have ears.'

Ava's hands were on her hips, her expression fierce. 'Yeah, tell the clue to the whole world, why don't you?' She turned on Miss Watson. 'I told you these kids would be a liability.'

Samia bristled. 'You're a kid too. And you're more bother than Frankie and me, with your constant moaning, and your noisy wheelie-case.'

Frankie burst out laughing. 'Burn.' He turned to Miss

Watson. 'I need to get this story straight in my heid. You've got a top-secret clue to solve, an Ava knows aw about it, an Samia an me have been dragged into this cos?'

For a moment, Miss Watson didn't reply. She was staring upwards, towards the entrance. Then she tutted, and waved a hand, as if midges were bothering her. 'I do believe someone is trailing us.'

Samia caught a glimpse of purple through the glass, and knew who it was right away.

'Yes, it's the old woman,' Samia confirmed. 'The one in the tartan cape who spoke to me on the train. She was following us and I reckon she knows we're in here.'

Miss Watson tutted again. 'We need to move quickly.'

'But last night, when Gabrielle... I thought... you said...' Ava spluttered.

'We have only eliminated one problem. There are clearly others. Let's go. This place is a maze of inter-connecting galleries. We should be able to shake this person off if we leave by one of the other exits.'

'But we can't leave until we solve the clue, can we?' Ava's voice sounded almost panicky. 'Otherwise, we won't know where to go next.'

'True. But it will take us too long to check every one of the art works in the Louvre. I'd hoped to have worked it out by now...'

Frankie and Samia glanced at each other. Their tour of Paris seemed to be sliding out of Miss Watson's control. But, lacking a viable alternative, they followed her and Ava as they hurried up to the first floor and dashed through the Denon gallery, stopping for a quick look at the Mona Lisa, which was barely visible through the jostling crowd.

'The Mona Lisa,' Miss Watson gave her own, enigmatic half-smile. 'Is one of the most valuable paintings in the world.'

'Millions an millions for a teeny wee picture like that!' Frankie scoffed. 'They was robbed. That other yin over there's better value. It's mahoosive and it's got a bit more action an aw.'

Miss Watson looked round at the picture at which Frankie was pointing. 'Size and amount of action aren't the usual ways of assessing a painting's worth, Frankie.'

She was about to say more, but Samia had spotted a small, tartan-draped figure at the other end of the long gallery.

'The old woman,' Samia gasped. 'She's here! Over there, see?'

'Right, let's move on. Quickly now, but don't arouse suspicion.'

Their whirlwind visit continued in the Sully Gallery, with its rows of Greek and Roman marble statues.

'Aw man. That's gross,' moaned Ava. 'Bare bums and willies everywhere.'

'Don't be such a Philistine,' snapped Miss Watson,

who looked pale and tired, and no wonder, after all the darting about she'd been doing in the other gallery, checking every label and sign, clearly desperate to try and solve this mysterious clue.

'Maybe we can help you, Miss Watson, if you slow down for a minute, and let us all think,' Samia suggested. 'Come on, guys. Small planet putting on his shoes. What can that mean?'

Frankie slumped down on a marble pedestal, causing one of the security men to come running, shooing him off.

'*Hé! Dégage!*'

'I'm getting up. Keep your hair on, wee man.' Frankie got to his feet, and started to list planets. 'Well, if we're talking toaty wee, there's the dwarf planets—Pluto, Ceres, Eris, Haumea, an the other yins. An if you're meaning the smallest planets in the solar system that would be Mercury, Venus and Earth.'

'Venus is over there!' Eyes gleaming, Ava pointed to the famous statue of the Venus de Milo.

'She looks *armless*,' sniggered Frankie.

'Yes, she. The clue says putting on his shoes,' Samia pointed out. 'So, it can't be referring to the statue of Venus.' A thought occurred to her. 'Wait a minute! Frankie, you said Mercury, didn't you?' She turned to Miss Watson. 'Wasn't Mercury the messenger of the gods? He was famous for his shoes! He wore winged sandals, didn't he?'

Miss Watson's face was glowing. 'Gracious, Samia. You're right... you've got it! And he's over there! Come on!'

Her heels clicked as she rushed across to a marble statue of a handsome, naked young man, his right foot resting on a rock while he fastened his sandal.

Miss Watson smiled approvingly. 'Hermes in Greek myth, Mercury to the Romans. The cleverest of the Olympians.'

Ava pulled a face. 'Not that smart. He's forgotten to put on his pants.'

'So...' Frankie scratched at his nose. 'We solved the clue. Do we get a prize?'

'No, we find the next clue. It will be around here somewhere.'

Not if the cleaners are doing their job, Samia thought gloomily, but she helped the others to look, searching all over the statue, while the security guard eyed them.

'It's there, I can see it.' Ava's voice was shaking. 'See the cloth, draped over his leg? There's a tiny scrap of blue paper stuck in that fold. Get it, Frankie.'

But it was Miss Watson who stretched out a hand and plucked the scrap of paper from Mercury's marble thigh. Then she turned to the children and smiled a bright smile.

'Well done. Excellent teamwork, I must say.' She popped the paper into her handbag and smiled again. 'We haven't seen all the art works, but I think that's enough for one morning. And I don't know about you children, but I'm ravenous. Let us go and buy some baguettes and have a lovely picnic in Tuileries Gardens. Doesn't that sound a marvellous idea?'

It did sound rather marvellous, Samia had to admit, as they trailed after Miss Watson towards one of the Louvre's side exits. She'd seen more than enough Madonna and Child paintings and bare-naked statues for one day, and was keen to be outside in the sunshine and fresh air. But, even though there was no sign of the old lady, and Samia kept glancing back to check, she had a horrible suspicion that Miss Watson was in a hurry because she knew they were still being followed.

Why would anyone be interested in chasing us around Paris? she wondered, as they stepped out into glorious sunshine. *Who's leaving clues for Miss Watson to follow, and why? What does the second clue say? And where are we travelling to next?*

There were so many unanswered questions, and the situation was so peculiar, that she felt a bit overwhelmed and afraid. But at the same time, the buzz of being on a real-life quest, even one spiced with danger, was electrifying. Samia was an avid reader, and she loved adventure stories, even the olden-day ones by Enid Blyton.

My parents told me this trip would be the adventure of a lifetime, but I don't expect this is quite what they had in mind.

6

THE SPY WHO DIED

The Jardin de Tuileries was more formal than Samia had expected. The neatly trimmed lawns were out of bounds for picnics, but they walked along gravel paths under manicured trees until they came to a large pond. There were quite a few people around, sitting on benches or on green metal chairs, chatting and enjoying the sunshine while their small children ran about on the grass.

Miss Watson had stopped at a stall on the way to purchase their lunch and she instructed the children to fetch four of the metal chairs from the stacks by the pond.

'Oh, this is splendid,' she said, sitting back in her chair, a pair of oversized sunglasses shielding her eyes. Despite the warm sunshine, she looked enviably cool, in her uncrumpled linen dress, and totally unfazed by all the drama at the Louvre. Without any fuss, she passed out a half baguette, filled with cheese and salad, a carton of fresh orange juice, a pear and a bar of chocolate to each of them. 'Eat and relax. We will have a chat about… everything, after lunch.'

The picnic was delicious, and the weather was perfect, sunny and warm with only a small, cooling breeze that stirred the leaves on the trees and rippled the pond. Samia found herself almost dozing off, head tilted back, enjoying the feel of the sun on her face, listening to the whoops of the children sailing their toy boats in the pond.

And then Miss Watson began to speak.

'As you can probably tell, caring for children is not my usual line of work.' She paused and cleared her throat. 'I'm a spy for MI6, and I am here in Europe on a mission.'

When Frankie gasped, an explosion of cheese and breadcrumbs shot from his mouth. 'Are you kiddin us on?'

Miss Watson waved her hand dismissively. 'Francis, please don't interrupt. Let me explain and then you may ask as many questions as you like. Within reason, and strict time limitations.'

Samia sat forward in her chair, desperate to get everything straight in her head. Frankie's face was funny; his eyes wide, mouth hanging open, the remains of his baguette abandoned to the sparrows. In contrast, Ava was leaning so far back in her chair that it was balanced on two legs. She was gazing up at the fluffy white clouds drifting across the sky, her face expressionless.

'Griff Fletcher was one of our best operatives.' Miss Watson's dark glasses hid her eyes, but there was a tiny break in her voice, and Samia suspected something awful had happened to Griff Fletcher. 'He'd spent the last six months undercover in Europe, infiltrating a small, but deadly group of neo-nazis. His work had been highly effective, and without arousing suspicion, he'd managed to reduce the size and effectiveness of the group, by sending the local police anonymous tip offs about the members' various illegal activities, causing them to be arrested and imprisoned.

'Even when there were just a few members remaining, suspicion only fell on Fletcher when he downloaded some top-secret intelligence from a group member's computer. He was caught in the act, and cover blown, he fled. Our last contact with Fletcher was a phone call from a public phone box, to say he was being tailed and would have to go on the run. He said he'd keep moving round Europe and leave a paper trail at various landmarks, a trail that would help lead us to the intelligence. He knew he was in terrible danger and was unlikely to survive. Griff Fletcher was a hero.'

Her voice cracked again, and Samia felt sad for her, because she had a suspicion Miss Watson had been very fond of Griff Fletcher.

'After that call, all contact stopped. He'd gone missing in action. And we had no idea of the whereabouts of the evidence he'd downloaded. And then, an envelope arrived at HQ, containing a postcard of the Louvre and the first clue. I was given the task of following this lead, but obviously the situation is a dangerous one and I needed a watertight cover story. And that's where your involvement began. Who would suspect me of spying if I were accompanied by three school children on their prize winners' trip around Europe?' She smiled brightly.

'And of course, I had another reason too, for inviting you along. My winners were carefully chosen. Samia, you are clearly academically bright and have excellent knowledge of art and history. Also, your essay was outstanding... very persuasive. As was yours Frankie... and your science knowledge has already proved vital. I am certain your language skills will prove useful too.'

Frankie nodded. 'Aye, I should be able to order a McDonald's just about anywhere.'

When Ava spoke, her voice was swamped in misery. 'If I'd written an essay, it would have been terrible. I'm ace at maths, but pure rubbish at English.'

A thought started buzzing, wasp-like, in Samia's brain.

But... if Ava didn't even enter the competition, how come she was one of the prize winners?

Miss Watson tutted and waved her hand at Ava, 'Your maths and logic skills will be invaluable. Without your coding skills, we wouldn't have been able to board the train. You are essential to the success of this operation.'

Samia had been floating in a little bubble of pleasure, repeating Miss Watson's words in her head: *academically bright; excellent knowledge of art and history; outstanding essay...*

But she couldn't let her critical thinking skills be smothered by a fluffy blanket of flattery. Pushing her hair back from her face, so she could look Miss Watson straight in the eye, she spoke in an accusing tone. 'You said nobody would suspect you, but you were wrong. What about the man on the train last night?'

Miss Watson nodded, as if in approval. 'Yes, that's true. According to Gabrielle, he has been a regular passenger on the London to Paris route recently, and no doubt he has been attempting to interrogate his fellow passengers during all those trips. He is a member of the neo-nazi group, who are clearly very keen to get to the evidence Griff has hidden before we do. But, as I said, Gabrielle has eliminated that particular problem.'

But there are others. And they're already on our trail...

Miss Watson's voice broke through Samia's thoughts.

'Anyway, that is the situation in which we find ourselves. There is a tiny, almost imperceptible element of risk, but any risk will be utterly outweighed by the educational benefits of our European adventure. So, will we carry on with our tour of beautiful Paris right now? We still have a lot to see!'

Samia's mind was still whirling. She had so many questions. But Frankie got in first.

'Haud on a minute. We found the clue! Are you no goin to tell us what it says?'

Miss Watson tapped her watch face. 'Not now. We are taking another train this evening and will have plenty of time to work on the clue then.'

'How do you know where we've to go next?' asked Samia. 'There was no postcard with this clue.'

'I know, child, because I took the liberty of unfolding the paper when I went to the ladies' room in the Louvre. I couldn't make head nor tail of the clue but there was a rough drawing of a bear on the other side. So, obviously—'

'We're going to Bern!' Samia clasped her hands tight, trying to contain her burst of joy. 'It has a medieval Old Town and a weird fountain with a child-eating ogre! It'll be amazing!'

Ava's eyes flicked open. 'And a bear, I'm guessing?' Her smile was almost invisible, but it was there, and Samia felt warmed by it.

'Lots of bears. On their flag and their buildings, but real bears too. They used to keep them in a bear pit, which sounds really cruel, but they're in a lovely park now, which is an improvement, I guess.'

'There are wild bears in the forests in Europe.' Ava stood up and stretched. 'I don't know why they're kept in captivity in Bern, just because the city's named after a bear.'

'Aye, that's no right. Shower o numpties. We could set the berrs free, while we're there.' Frankie was grinning, but Samia didn't doubt he'd have a go.

'You'll do no such thing!' Miss Watson looked alarmed. 'The bears are perfectly content in captivity, I'm sure.'

'Are we getting on the Euro Métro again?' asked Samia, getting to her feet, and gathering up the rubbish strewn round their chairs.

'Yes, we are. Bern doesn't have a subway system, but there's a Euro Métro halt under the main railway station, and the service is much more regular in mainland Europe than it is in the UK. Come along now, we have more of Paris to see first!'

After re-stacking their chairs and putting the picnic remnants in the bin, they left the Jardin de Tuileries. Samia's heart felt light as she walked towards with the others.

Miss Watson's right. We can just focus on having a great time, visiting European cities and solving clues along the way. And we'll be moving around so often that the baddies, whoever they are, won't be able to keep up.

But then a horrible thought burst her happy bubble.

Moving around didn't work for Griff Fletcher. They obviously caught up with him... and then he vanished.

WHERE ARE WE?

1. THIS COUNTRY IS LANDLOCKED. IT HAS NO COASTLINE.

2. THE NATIONAL FLAG IS SQUARE, RATHER THAN RECTANGULAR.

3. THIS COUNTRY HAS FOUR OFFICIAL LANGUAGES.

7

THE BABY-EATING OGRE

By the time they got onto the Euro Métro heading for Bern, Frankie had lost his Tigger-like bounce, Ava was moaning about her blistered heel and Samia felt weak with tiredness. Only Miss Watson was still marching along at her usual pace in her sensible court shoes, linen dress still miraculously uncrushed, lipstick still bright, hair neatly brushed.

They'd had a brilliant afternoon, negotiating the sights of Paris. For Samia, the highlight was the Jardins du Trocadéro. Frankie had got soaked at the Fountain of Warsaw, a massive mirror-like basin in which multiple fountains shot water skyward. Ava had decided they should all have a go on the carousel in the park and even Miss Watson had got onto one of the horses. As they'd twirled round, all of them shrieking with laughter, clutching tightly to the spiralled poles, in case they slid off their horses' slippery saddles, Samia had reflected that this was a moment she'd remember, even when the memories of all the magnificent statues, artwork and buildings had gone.

Their last stop had been the Eiffel Tower and Miss Watson had insisted they walk up the 700 steps to the second floor, rather than taking the lift, which was probably why they were all so shattered.

The train to Bern was identical to the one they'd boarded in Glasgow, and luckily, the password hadn't changed. Although it was busier, they found a table easily. Samia scanned the carriage, still checking for the presence of the old lady, but she wasn't there.

The other passengers were a group of smartly dressed young men, sitting at two adjoining tables, talking into their phones instead of to each other, and three women in stylish suits, who'd clearly combined business with a shopping trip, as the spare seat was piled high with bags.

Perhaps the old lady isn't following us after all. Maybe my imagination's gone into overdrive, because of all this spy stuff.

The thought reminded her of the clue, still tucked in Miss Watson's bag, but when she mentioned it, Miss Watson insisted they wait until after dinner.

Samia had believed she was too tired to eat, but she rallied when dinner arrived, brought by a waiter with neatly combed black hair and immaculate chef's whites. A delicious tomatoey smell wafted into her nostrils.

'Oh, cassoulet!' exclaimed Miss Watson, as an earthenware dish was placed in front of her.

Frankie peered into his own dish. 'Also known as

beans an sausage,' he murmured.

It was only after they'd polished off their chocolate gateaux and ice cream, that Miss Watson finally produced the crumpled scrap of blue paper.

'Okay, children. Thinking caps on.'

Ava rolled her eyes so hard you could only see the whites, which was totally gross and made Samia feel a bit sick, though her nausea might have been caused by the cassoulet and gateau sloshing around in her stomach as the train rattled along through endless dark tunnels.

It doesn't say much,' Miss Watson sighed, a little wistfully, as if she'd wished for a more personal message. *'Chronos hits.'*

Samia sat in silence, trying desperately to recall some Greek myths. 'Kronos… is he the guy who ate his kids?' Everyone else looked blank, so she retold as much of the story as she could remember. 'It's a really gruesome myth. Kronos was the last of the Titans. When he became the ruler of the universe, someone, I can't remember who, prophesised that one of his children would overthrow him, so he ate his babies as soon as they were born… except the last one.

Rhea, the babies' mum, was getting a bit hacked off about the whole baby-eating thing, so she gave Kronos a stone wrapped in a blanket, and told him it was their baby, who she'd hidden in a cave. He swallowed the stone, and the actual baby—Zeus—grew up and overthrew his father, once he'd got him to sick up all his siblings.'

Ava pulled a face. 'Samia, that's gross.'

'Yeah, I told you it was horrible.' An idea came to her. 'Wait! Do you think the next clue's on the fountain in Bern with the child-eating ogre? That would make sense wouldn't it?'

Miss Watson smiled. 'Well done, Samia. I am extremely glad I brought you along on this trip. Your knowledge is proving very useful.'

'Aye, it's just as well.' Frankie grinned good-naturedly and helped himself to the last slice of gateau. 'I didn't have a clue about that yin.'

'Google would have done the same thing quicker,' Ava snapped, and Samia didn't even look at her, in case she was doing another eye-roll.

She felt fuzzy with tiredness, and was glad when Miss Watson suggested they find their cabins for the night. As she followed the others towards the front carriage she noticed that two of the ladies had left, leaving one sitting alone with all the shopping bags. When she walked past, the lone woman grasped her wrist.

'Are you four from Scotland?' Her voice was rich and deep, her accent French. Her auburn hair fell round her shoulders in glamorous waves. She was wearing a bright pink jacket, and thick-lensed glasses which magnified her eyes. 'I adore those cute accents!'

'Samia, smile!' Frankie was standing in the aisle,

holding up his disposable camera. The woman dropped Samia's arm, just as Frankie clicked.

'We're on a school trip,' said Samia, moving away as she spoke. 'With our teacher.'

She felt uncomfortable about the exchange, partly because her sleeve had been grabbed by a total stranger, and partly because it was yet another person showing an interest in their trip. It felt as though spies were everywhere.

But the night passed without incident, and when the train pulled into the halt on schedule the next morning, Samia felt refreshed, and excited about their visit to the Swiss capital. She just wished Ava would show even a tiny bit of enthusiasm and wondered for about the tenth time why she'd come on this trip and how she'd won the prize in the first place.

As the three deposited their luggage, and followed Miss Watson out of Bern's railway station she decided to broach the subject.

'Ava, how come you're here, on this trip? If you didn't enter the competition, I mean?'

'Samia, does it ever occur to you to just stop talking and mind your own blooming business?' There was a short painful silence, before Ava spoke again. 'I didn't say I didn't enter the competition. I just didn't write an essay. I produced a video, with music and sound effects and everything. Miss Watson thought it was genius. She said it made her cry.'

'Oh… that's nice.' Samia didn't know what else to say. She was feeling a bit crushed, to be honest. Miss Watson hadn't said *her* essay was genius.

Frankie burst out laughing. 'Samia, you've got a face like a skelped bum. Your competitive streak's as wide as the Clyde.'

Samia felt her face flush and when she spoke, she didn't like the defensive note in her voice. 'There's nothing wrong with being competitive. My dad says it keeps you motivated to improve.'

'Aye, but as my maw says, *other folk doin well doesn't hurt you.* Build folk up. There's no need to knock them doon.'

Ava grinned, a genuine smile that lit her face. 'Frankie's right, you know. You need to change your mindset. Other people don't have to lose for you to win.'

Miss Watson's voice rang out, every syllable clearly enunciated. 'Shall we focus on the present, children? What do you think of beautiful Bern?'

Samia blinked. She'd been so busy thinking about what Frankie had said that she hadn't really been aware of her surroundings. But now she realised they'd been dropped into the setting of a fairy tale. A city of ancient stone buildings with orange octagonal roof tiles, arches, arcades and fountains, Bern was the very definition of picturesque. They went through an arch to the left of the grand Parliament building and Miss Watson pointed out the Alps in the distance and the blue-green river below.

'It's all so sparkly clean,' sighed Samia wistfully. 'No litter or graffiti anywhere.'

Ava pulled a face. 'Yeah, it's spotless. But it's not exactly edgy.'

'Switzerland does tend to veer away from the bold and unconventional.' Miss Watson smiled. 'But it does picture-perfect very nicely. Even the water from the fountains is completely safe to drink!'

'Speaking of those, should we go and find the child-eating ogre fountain and get the clue?' said Samia.

'We'll have a good look around the city first.' Miss Watson seemed perfectly relaxed, wearing a pretty pink floral dress, topped by a light lemon cardigan with mother-of-pearl buttons. It was a mystery how she managed to dress so beautifully, in a fresh, perfectly ironed outfit every day.

They walked the cobbled streets for ages, taking photos of the cathedral and of Albert Einstein's house, much to Frankie's joy.

'Albert freakin Einstein… take a photie o me chappin the big man's front door.'

Afterwards, they had hot chocolate and apple pie with cream in a pretty café and wandered through the covered shopping arcades, before finally ending up at the *Kindlifresserbrunnen* fountain.

It was without doubt the most grotesque sculpture Samia had ever seen. The ogre sat at the top of a plinth, the bottom half of a small child dangling from his gaping jaws. Four more clearly terrified children were stuffed in a sack in his hand, presumably for eating later.

'That statue's minging. Are they tryin to give their weans nightmares?' grumbled Frankie, while he inspected the base, trying to locate the hidden clue. But he was having no luck, and neither were the others.

'Maybe someone cleared the clue away.' Ava slumped on to the fountain's stone base, her face gloomy. 'That piece of paper would have been the only scrap of litter in Bern, after all.'

Samia plonked herself down beside Ava, a feeling of despair settling like fog.

Is this the end? If we can't find the clue, will Miss Watson give up and go home? It has to be somewhere on the fountain. Kronos hits...

A horrible thought struck her like a blow to the stomach, and she leant forward, tears stinging her eyes.

Oh, no. Oh no... oh no... have I got this all wrong?

8

CLUE O'CLOCK

Samia brushed tears of frustration and shame from her eyes and looked up at Miss Watson. 'Please, can I look at the last clue? I think I might have made a tiny mistake.'

When Miss Watson handed her the paper, Samia realised what had happened right away. Anxiety tightened in her chest. *They're going to think I'm a total idiot.*

But she had to tell them. They were all looking at her, waiting for her to continue.

'I'm so sorry, guys. I've got the wrong God. Kronos with a K was the baby-eating Titan. This clue refers to Chronos with a C. In Greek mythology he's the personification of time. I'm so, so sorry.'

'So you should be.' Ava's voice was scratchy with annoyance. 'We've been paddling about in this freaking nightmare fountain and we should be hunting at that big clock instead? The big clock we walked past half an hour ago?'

Frankie waded back from the middle of the fountain, where he'd been inspecting the circle of bears at the base, and clambered out.

'Ava, keep your hair on. It's no exactly a world-ending disaster. You've no even got wet, have you?'

The look Ava gave him should have frozen him like Mr Tumnus in Narnia, but Frankie seemed totally unfazed. While he pulled his socks back on and laced up his trainers, Miss Watson checked the Bern tourist guide she'd picked up at the station.

'There's a tour of the inside of the clock tower just before two pm. Let's walk up to the Rosengarten, have some lunch and then we can go to the Zytglogge, and hopefully, we'll be able to locate the clue there.' She patted Samia's hand. 'Don't look so upset, Samia. It wasn't your fault. I should have showed you the paper and am totally to blame.'

The words *totally to blame* reverberated in Samia's brain during the walk uphill from the old Bear Pit to the Rose Garden. She could feel Ava's anger pulsating, and Miss Watson kept checking her watch.

What if I'm wrong? What will happen if we can't find the clue?

'There's a berr.' Frankie pointed towards the Bear Pit, where a massive brown bear was ambling out of the tunnel connecting the old pit with the new larger enclosure.

But the sight of the animal just deepened Samia's gloom. 'He should be free to roam. Unicorns are Scotland's national animal and we don't keep *them* in captivity.'

'Fair point.' Frankie grinned at her, and she tried to

smile back, but by the time they'd eaten a picnic lunch in the Rose Garden and admired the stunning views of the beautiful city and winding turquoise river below them, she was completely on edge, and could think of nothing else but getting to the clock tower and proving to them all that she hadn't made another mistake.

As they headed back downhill towards the Zytglogge, Ava fell into step beside her. Frankie and Miss Watson were striding ahead.

'Samia, look, I'm sorry. I was too hard on you earlier. Miss Watson's right. It wasn't your fault. And Frankie was right too… the rest of us didn't have the faintest idea.' Ava paused. 'It's just that…'

Her voice tailed away, because a woman had stepped into their path. Recognising her at once, by her long auburn hair and owl-like glasses, Samia gasped.

It's the nosey woman who grabbed my wrist on the train.

The woman was wearing the same tailored pink jacket and well-designed black trousers, with an expensive camera slung round her neck. She was smiling brightly, showing even white teeth, looking totally normal.

'Excuse me, girls. I was hoping you could show me the way to the Rose Garden. I've heard the views are beautiful.'

'Just keep going straight uphill. It's as boring as it sounds though.' Ava stepped forward, clearly expecting the stranger to move aside, but she stayed exactly where she was.

'Thank you. I'm a visitor here, like yourselves...' She paused and peered at Ava through those thick-lensed glasses. 'What brings you to Bern?'

'We're on a school trip. That's our teacher, down the hill. She's waiting for us.'

'Teacher, is she? What school?'

'West Parkland High.' Ava's lie was smooth as butter.

'Bern is not a usual destination for school trips.' The woman's voice was ice-cold and Samia realised she'd lost the delightful French accent she'd had last night. 'I think you're lying.'

'No, we're not! We're doing a tour of capital cities,' Samia broke in, her voice rising to a squeak.

'Yeah, and Bern's a capital city.' Ava took hold of Samia's arm. 'We need to go. Let us past.'

Ava tried to dodge around the woman, pulling Samia with her, but as she stepped to the right the woman did the same, and then just as quickly to the left. Anxiety quivered in Samia's stomach. The pavement was narrow, and the road busy with traffic. They were trapped, and there was something really scary about the stranger's owl-like stare.

Is she one of the people who are trying to find the information Griff Fletcher has hidden? Does she suspect that Miss Watson's a spy?

As Samia watched, panic rising, the woman reached into the pocket of her jacket, and Ava went crazy.

'Get lost, you freak! Let us past!' she yelled, kicking hard. As Ava's Doc Marten crashed into her shin, the woman howled. Without waiting another second, Ava started to run, dragging Samia behind her, hurtling down the hill towards Miss Watson and Frankie.

'We need to move quickly,' Ava panted, grabbing Frankie's arm. 'We need to find the clue and get out of Bern. They're on our tail.'

Miss Watson remained unruffled, her voice as cool as the water in Bern's fountains.

'Don't worry, children. I am quite sure we can stay a step or two ahead.'

As they headed into the Old Town's narrow cobbled alleys, Samia's heart was racing, but she felt weak with relief to have escaped, and grateful to Ava for saving them both.

They arrived just as the Zytglogge struck the hour, and stared upwards as a colourful jester and a line of bears paraded across the clock front. A golden Chronos turned the hourglass and opened his mouth as the bell rang. As a gilded rooster lifted its wings and crowed, Miss Watson clapped her hands. 'How utterly charming!'

Beside her, an old man spoke. '*Gnädiga Frau, entshuldigen sie bitte...*' He turned to the children, and smiled. 'I am the Governor of Time, responsible for this incredible clock. Albert Einstein was gazing up at this very clocktower when he first came up with his theory of relativity. The Zytglogge helped change the way we think about the universe. Come inside the watchtower to see more!'

As Miss Watson bought tickets, Frankie chatted away to the man in German.

'Come along, Francis. You'll hear all about Einstein during the tour, I'm sure.'

Miss Watson sounded totally composed, but as they headed inside, Samia noticed her glancing behind, checking they weren't being followed.

The elderly man guided them up a twisting narrow staircase inside the medieval watchtower, into a stone-walled room. Most of the space was taken up by an intricate iron construction; a mass of cogs, gears and levers, powered by a huge pendulum. As the old man pointed out the workings of the clock, the loud tick, steady as a heartbeat, made him hard to hear. And even if they'd all been fascinated by clockwork, they had a job to do.

Frankie was standing so close to the clock's apparatus that he was in danger of getting his jacket sleeve entangled in the moving machinery. Together, Ava and Samia checked the crevices in the stonework, feeling with their fingers, while trying to fake interest in the man's explanations and not attract the attention of the other tourists in the crowded room. Miss Watson had removed her sunglasses and although she was standing very still, head tilted as if she was concentrating on every word, her eyes were darting, checking the gaps in the floor.

But time was passing, its steady tick inescapable here, and Samia's anxiety was rising.

We aren't going to find the clue here either. It's over.

Once his talk ended, the tour guide led them up further narrow stairs to the monument's viewing platform. When Frankie gave a loud gasp, Samia thought at first he was scared by the height, or just overwhelmed by the incredible view of the city. But when she looked over, Frankie's grin was triumphant. He was waving a clenched fist, and as they clustered round him, he uncurled his hand. Samia sighed with relief when she saw a tightly folded scrap of blue paper lying in his palm.

'It was jammed into a wee gap in the stonework,' crowed Frankie. 'I nearly missed it!'

Before the breeze could send the scrap of paper scudding over Bern's rooftops and spires, Miss Watson took it from Frankie's hand and popped it in her bag, her smile as wide as the Cheshire Cat's.

'Well done, Francis. Now, I think our tour of the Zytglogge is over. Let us head to a café and find out where we are travelling next.'

In the café, they shared a celebration chocolate fondue,

and as Samia dipped yet another delicious strawberry into warm, gooey chocolate, she felt a glow of happiness. Then she realised Ava was watching her, and wondered if she'd been a bit greedy with the strawberries.

'You okay now?' Ava asked. 'I thought you were going to explode with stress this afternoon, and it made me feel really bad, because you're doing your best, and you didn't ask to get mixed up in this.'

Samia popped the strawberry in her mouth, to give herself time to think. At home, doing her best rarely felt good enough. Her older sister Shanaz was studying medicine and Samia couldn't seem to rid herself of the feeling that her sister was the clever one, and that *she* would never manage to do as well, and make her parents proud. But now she thought about it, although her mum and dad *were* massively proud of Shanaz, they never made comparisons and they were always supportive— they'd taken her out for pizza when she'd won the History Hero certificate. If she was being totally honest, the pressure she put on herself was mostly self-inflicted.

She smiled at Ava. 'Yeah, I'm fine now thanks. And thanks for rescuing me this afternoon.'

Ava shrugged. 'Ha, that was mainly about self-preservation. I thought the crazy cow was going for a weapon.'

Frankie held up his wooden skewer, dripping melted chocolate on to the white lace tablecloth. 'These wee chibs would have come in handy. I'm goin to tuck one inside my jaikit.'

'Not that one, eejit. Take a clean one.' Ava handed him a skewer from the pile beside the fondue set.

'We make a pretty good team, don't we?' said Samia, just as the click of heels behind her announced Miss Watson's return from the ladies' room.

Frankie nodded. 'Aye. We should have a team name—'

'I think not.' Miss Watson plonked herself down on a seat. 'Are you all finished? I've checked the note. Griff has done a rather appalling drawing of a wolf so I am fairly certain I know where we are travelling to next—'

Releasing a squeal, Samia clasped her hands together. 'Oh, there's a she-wolf in the story of Romulus and Remus!'

'Shush, Samia!' Ava glanced around at the café's other customers and lowered her own voice to a whisper. 'What's the clue?'

Miss Watson sighed. 'It means absolutely nothing to me.' Her next words were almost inaudible. *'Skate around downstairs.'*

Eyes bright with hope, Miss Watson looked around the table, but if their blank expressions were anything to go by, both Ava and Frankie shared Samia's feelings of total bafflement.

Frankie sighed. 'Haven't the foggiest. Just as well we didn't bother wi a team name. We're scuppered.'

'Now, Francis. Let's not be too negative. Perhaps all will become as clear as crystal once we are in the midst of the Eternal City. Come along children. The Euro Métro leaves in half an hour.' Miss Watson checked her phone and *tsked*. 'Oh heavens, there's a new code word to find—K Z G G V I M. Ava?'

She passed the phone to Ava, and the girl stared, unblinking, at the letters and then passed it back with a sigh.

'Again, far too easy to crack. It's an Atbash Cipher. Simple alphabet reversal. Honestly, can't they come up with trickier codes?'

As they left the café, Ava walked beside Samia.

'When we get there, don't stress if you can't work out the landmark clue and don't pay any attention to me if I get snappy. I'll be angry at myself, not at you.'

Samia slipped her arm through Ava's. 'Well, you should try and relax a bit too. Don't get mad at yourself. As you said, we can only do our best and we didn't ask to get mixed up in this.'

Ava pulled away from Samia. When she spoke, there was real despair in her voice. 'But I *did*, and I *need* us to succeed.'

69

WHERE ARE WE?

1. THIS COUNTRY HAS THREE ACTIVE VOLCANOES.

2. THE NATIONAL FLAG IS RED, WHITE AND GREEN.

3. THIS COUNTRY IS SHAPED LIKE A HIGH-HEELED BOOT KICKING A BALL.

9

DEATH IN THE HOUSE

The following morning, well rested after a night's sleep in her cosy cabin, Samia tucked into a delicious breakfast of *cornetti* filled with *marmellata*, basically the Italian version of croissants and jam, and then got off the Euro Métro with the others.

As they exited the Termini Train Station, Samia was hit in the face by a chaotic hubbub of sound, heat and movement. Scooters weaved crazily between buses, car horns blasted and crowds of tourists surged along the pavements. Rome seemed like bedlam after Bern's serene orderliness, and it was exhilarating.

'Stay close!' demanded Miss Watson, looking glamorous in a swirly cotton frock, sandals and enormous sunhat. 'And follow me!'

As they approached the Colosseum, Samia felt a tingle of excitement. It was incredible to think that this building had been around for two thousand years.

'Now, here we are in Ancient Rome!' Miss Watson announced as they approached the Colosseum. 'This arena was where people came to watch gruesome spectacles, like wild animals fighting to the death, gladiators locked in battle and public executions.'

Samia squinted at the Colosseum's gigantic columns, trying to imagine that she really was living in Ancient Rome, but then Frankie spoiled it by pointing out yet another branch of McDonald's.

They kept walking, jostled by the crowds, down the Via dei Fori Imperiali to admire the Trevi Fountain.

'That's a lot less nightmare-inducing than the baby-eating ogre fountain,' said Ava. 'I like the horses and the merfolk.'

'Actually, they're Tritons, not mermen, but yes, it is a very attractive fountain. Legend says that if you throw a coin into the Trevi Fountain, you will return to Rome one day, so perhaps we ought to do that?' said Miss Watson.

'Or I could fish aw the coins out?' suggested Frankie, a hopeful glint in his eye. 'I could do with the cash.'

'Indeed, you will not. The coins are gathered up and given to charity.'

They watched other tourists tossing coins in the fountain first, and there appeared to be a specific method.

'Okay, so you're meant to face away from the fountain, and throw the coin with your right hand, over your left shoulder,' said Samia. 'Got that, Frankie?'

Frankie's coin spun, hit a Triton in the face, and plopped into the water. Raising both hands, he started chanting,

so loudly other tourists turned to look. '*Championes!*
Championes! I'm comin back to freakin Rome!'

They all had a go, and as Samia threw her coin, she
made a wish, that she too might return one day to this
magnificent city, with its incredible history and beautiful
buildings in their glorious sunset colours. Luckily, the
coin splashed into the fountain on her third attempt.

Afterwards, they walked up the Spanish Steps to the
big church at the top.

'Jeez, I'm pure puggled,' Frankie grumbled. '135
steps... what were they eejits thinkin?'

Even Miss Watson looked a little weary. 'The steps
were built to link the piazza with this magnificent church.'
She took off her wide-brimmed hat and fanned her face.
'But I sense we're all a little too hot and bothered to focus
on history. Let's go back down and get a cool drink and
a *gelato*.'

'Yay!' Ava started hurrying down the steps, and was
almost at the bottom when she tripped and tumbled
down the rest of the stairs. Samia gasped in horror, her
hand flying to her face.

'Ava!' she yelled, rushing towards the crumpled figure.
By the time she reached the bottom of the steps, a small
crowd had gathered. Miss Watson elbowed them aside,
her voice ringing out above the sympathetic chatter. 'Let
me through, please. I am the girl's guardian. Ava, are you
hurt, child?'

Looking rather dazed, Ava got to her feet, aided by Samia and Frankie, while Miss Watson shooed the onlookers away.

'Aw, this is mortifying. Let's get away from here,' Ava muttered. Her face glowed scarlet, and she was gritting her teeth, clearly trying not to cry. Supported by Samia, she limped a few metres, but then stopped and stared up at the building on the right of the steps.

'Hey, look at that! *K-E-A-T-S*... Those are the same letters as the ones on the blue paper!'

Miss Watson looked worried. 'Do you think the child has concussion? Maybe we should take her to the hospital.'

But Frankie's eyes were gleaming. 'No, she's right! They're the same letters, just in a different order. The clue's an anagram! Look!'

They all looked at the big sign on the side of the building.

The Keats-Shelley Memorial House

'See!' Frankie was dancing from foot to foot, delighted with their discovery. '*Skate around downstairs*! Keats is an anagram of *skate* an his hoose is at the bottom of these steps. The next clue's in there!'

Miss Watson smiled. 'Good work, Francis. And well done, Ava. Even in a time of personal crisis, you have kept a clear head and retained your ability to solve puzzles. But let's have a *gelato* first. You need time to rest your ankle.'

It took a little while to find a café, and Ava's face was pale and strained by the time they located one down a quiet alley, with spare seats and shade and less astronomical prices than the ones in the main square. There were so many flavours of *gelato* available that it was almost impossible to choose. Samia picked a *coppa* with two scoops, one Amalfi lemon and the other coconut. Frankie chose mint and chocolate. Ava asked for a plain cone with one scoop of vanilla and sat so quietly, eyes half-closed, that Samia wondered if maybe she *had* banged her head.

It was so shady in the alley that Miss Watson took off her sunglasses, and as she sat in her wicker chair, sipping an iced-coffee, she looked perfectly relaxed.

'Do you see the girl in the hooded top, slouched in that shop doorway like a vagrant?' she said suddenly, her voice low. 'She has been following us since we arrived in Rome.'

Ava's eyes flicked open. 'Another one?' she groaned. 'Are they all part of this neo-nazi group, do you think?'

Miss Watson nodded. 'I believe they are.'

She sighed and placed her coffee down on the rickety table. 'I have kept some details from you all, but I think you need to understand who is involved, and what's at stake.'

'That would be good.' Frankie's attempt to look serious was rather spoiled by his chocolate moustache. Samia leaned forward, her heart thudding, as Miss Watson began to talk.

'On the London to Paris train, Gabrielle identified her assailant right away as William Malcoeur. Malcoeur, who is a British citizen, has been on MI6's radar for a long time. He and his sister, Marlena, along with her boyfriend, Victor Klein, have been involved in the neo-nazi movement for many years. About twelve years ago, furious about the EU's decision to implement diversity charters aimed at preventing discrimination, Victor, Marlena and William set up their own neo-nazi group, and spent several of the following years in prison for various offences. Victor died from natural causes while he was in jail, although Marlena claims he was assassinated. The group has made frequent threats to deface Europe's most famous cultural landmarks, unless the diversity charters are abandoned.'

'Marlena will be spittin teeth now her brother's deid an aw,' Frankie remarked.

'That unfortunate incident was self-defence. Malcoeur was armed and was about to discharge his weapon.' Miss Watson's reply was cool and practised, and Samia wondered how many times she had found herself in violent, dangerous situations. It wasn't hard to imagine her facing dangerous baddies with the same firm, unflappable approach she used with them.

Unclasping her handbag, Miss Watson pulled out a

photograph of a scowling, fair-haired woman.

'This is Marlena Malcoeur. She is in her mid-thirties and of medium build. I want you to look out for her, and if you see her, let me know immediately. She is *very* dangerous, but there are clearly other members still at large, despite Griff Fletcher's sterling efforts, and these people may well be equally dangerous.'

Ava's chair nearly toppled as she leant forward, and plucked the photograph from Miss Watson's fingers.

For a long moment, she stared at it, her eyes dark with anger.

'Evil cow,' she hissed, and Samia was startled by the venom in her voice.

Firmly, Miss Watson removed the photo from Ava's hand and placed it back in her bag.

Ava pushed her chair back with her feet, so far that it nearly toppled, tilted her face and half-closed her eyes.

Miss Watson glanced at Ava and frowned. 'You're very pale, child.' She turned to the others. 'Perhaps it would be best in the current circumstances if Ava remains here and rests for a moment, while the rest of us go in search of the next clue?'

Appalled, Samia opened her mouth to protest.

Ava's only twelve. You can't leave a twelve-year-old kid alone in a strange city!

But Ava was nodding in agreement, and Miss Watson was getting to her feet.

'Right, decision made. And Ava, it would be useful if you could check if the girl in the hooded top leaves at the same time as we do.'

Reluctantly, Samia stood up too, thoughts whirling as she tried to justify what they were about to do.

Ava doesn't look at all well. The fall must have given her a horrible shock. But maybe Miss Watson's right and it isn't fair to make her limp around a museum when she clearly needs to rest.

'We'll be back as soon as possible. I'll let the café staff know you're waiting here for a little while, and leave you money for a cool drink or another *gelato*. It will be absolutely fine.'

As Miss Watson handed Ava a twenty Euro note, Samia caught a flicker of anxiety in the woman's eyes. But then she put her sunglasses back on, and any evidence of doubt vanished.

Frankie seemed totally unfazed by the decision to leave Ava behind. He was bouncing on his toes, keen to be going clue-hunting again.

As they walked past the hunched, hooded figure in the alley, Samia took a closer look, but the girl's head was bent, long strands of greasy black hair hanging limply, and she'd pulled a blanket over her legs. It was hard to believe this pitiful soul was tracking them.

But as they turned out of the alley, she glanced behind, and saw the hooded figure scrambling to her feet.

'It's no a hoose at aw, it's a second-floor flat,' grumbled Frankie as they climbed the stairs of the Keats-Shelley Memorial House. Once inside though, he stopped complaining, as the rooms were blissfully cool. They skipped the introductory film about the lives and works of the Romantic Poets and hurried to the adjoining room, with its rows of glass cases displaying the poets' letters and documents. Miss Watson began looking inside the cases, but Frankie and Samia, who were closer to the next room, could hear the guide speaking to a tour group. And she was talking about Keats. Sliding into the room, they stood at the back and listened. 'In 1820 John Keats was very ill with tuberculosis and his doctors told him a warm climate might help to improve his health. Tragically, he died in this very room, aged only 25.'

Looking around the spartanly furnished room, with its narrow bed, Samia shivered, although that might have been because the powerful air-conditioning made the room chilly.

The tour guide was pointing out other items in the room. 'And you can see the poet's death mask, here on the wall.'

'A whit?' muttered Frankie. 'Aw, man. That's pure gross. Why would you want a plaster cast of a deid person's heid?'

The guide scowled at him, and ushered the tour group out.

'It's a perfectly legitimate question,' murmured Samia, to the guide's back. A little nervously, she moved closer to the death mask. The poet's eyes were closed and he appeared to be wearing a bandage on his head. It wasn't scary, not really… just awfully sad. Keats had only been a couple of years older than her big sister.

'Do you think the clue will be hidden on that… thing?' Frankie was standing well back, beside the poet's desk.

'Well, his name's the clue, and that's the closest we can get to the actual Keats.'

Listening out for the guide, Samia slid one hand under the case. Her fingers touched a small, sticky lump. 'Oh, double gross,' she hissed, shuddering. But there was crumpled paper there too, she could feel it, so she tugged. The blue scrap of paper was laced with sticky white strands, as the clue had clearly been stuck to the underside of the case with a blob of chewing gum.

'Oh, yuck. Thanks for that, Griff Fletcher.' Pulling a face, paper pinched between finger and thumb, she held it up so Frankie could see. He gave her a thumbs up, but made no attempt to take the clue.

'Ya beauty… I'll let you hold on to that yin.'

The window in Keats' bedroom was closed, and when she looked down, Samia could see the piazza, busy with people, and felt suddenly dizzy. Clutching the side of the window, she turned to Frankie. 'We need to get back to Ava. Now.'

'What's up?'

'I don't know. I just have a bad feeling. We need to go.'

In the other room, Miss Watson was peering at a letter in a glass case. When they rushed towards her, she gestured at them to slow down.

'Show some respect, children. Look at this item… a love letter from John Keats to his fiancée. Listen to this. *My dear Girl, I love you ever and ever and without reserve…* Oh, it's so tragic.' Miss Watson dabbed at her eyes with a tissue, and Samia wondered if she was thinking about Griff Fletcher, her own lost love.

'Can I borrow that hankie?' Samia wrapped the sticky blob in the tissue and handed it to Miss Watson. 'There's the clue, but you might want to wear gloves to unwrap it. Miss Watson, we need to go. Ava—'

'Ava will be perfectly fine, Samia. You worry too much.'

Maybe I do, but this isn't about winning prizes, or passing tests, or solving clues. This is about Ava, being all by herself when there are bad people about.

As Miss Watson said her goodbyes to the lady at the door of the museum, Samia was hopping from foot to foot, desperate to leave.

We've left Ava alone. Why's Miss Watson not hurrying? What if something terrible has happened to Ava?

Emerging from the cool quiet of the apartment into the clamour and bright sunlight of the Piazza de Spagna was a shock. But the second shock was far worse. Losing patience with Miss Watson and Frankie's slow pace, Samia pushed through the thronged piazza and rushed towards the alley. As she ran down the narrow lane, she could see their café, with its hanging sign and cheerful red awning. All of the round tables were occupied. At the table where they'd left Ava, a balding, middle-aged man was tucking into a bowlful of spaghetti with clams.

Ava was nowhere to be seen.

10

GIRL, MISSING

The man at the café table was studiously ignoring Samia, trying to focus on his *spaghetti alle vongele*, while she stared at him, open-mouthed, struggling to believe he was there, instead of Ava. Behind her, she heard Frankie shout.

'Miss Watson—Ava's no here!'

The heels of her sandals clacking on the cobbles, Miss Watson rushed into the café area, calling Ava's name. A waiter appeared, gesticulating wildly, clearly aghast at the fuss being made while customers were trying to enjoy their lunch. Frankie spoke to him urgently, in fluent Italian. When the waiter pointed down the alley, back the way they'd just come, the boy turned to Samia and Miss Watson, his forehead creased with worry. 'Apparently she left, just after we did.'

Miss Watson's hand flew to her mouth. 'What on earth was she thinking?'

Anger and fear churned in Samia's stomach.

What were YOU thinking?? You were meant to be looking after us. You left Ava all by herself!!

She didn't even try and disguise her sharp tone. 'I reckon she has gone after the homeless girl in the hoodie. After all, you *did* tell Ava it would be useful if she could check up on her. Anything could have happened!'

Frankie put his hand on her arm. 'Ava'll be okay. She's no daft.'

Gulping, trying to hold back tears, Samia shook him off. 'Neither was Griff Fletcher, apparently, and he has never been seen again. We need to find Ava. Now. But how on earth will we know where she's gone? She could be anywhere! And Rome's huge!'

Frankie pointed at the gutter running along the side of the alley. Next to a drain, an arrow had been created from two iced-coffee straws. 'Just a wee hunch, but I figure she went left.'

Hope leapt in Samia's heart. 'Quick. Let's go!'

She sped off, Frankie and Miss Watson rushing along behind, pushing through the crowds at the bottom of the Spanish Steps, hurrying across the piazza.

'There's another arrow. Look!' Samia had no proof that the arrow, scratched on the cobbles with a stone, had been drawn by Ava, but it was the only clue they had, so they followed it down Via Frattini.

The street was lined with expensive-looking shops, and was crowded with sightseers. As she attempted to zig-zag through the hordes of people, all armed with bulky shopping bags, or intent on dawdling to gaze in shop windows, Samia could feel panic rising in her throat. When they passed an outdoor café, the pedestrians were funnelled into a narrower space, and she found her way blocked. It was like one of those awful nightmares, the ones where you're trying to get somewhere in a hurry, but your limbs have turned to jelly and every step seems to happen in slow-motion.

Frantically, she looked around for another arrow, but there was no sign of one. And even if Ava had drawn or made one on the ground, it would surely have been rubbed out or kicked apart by all those sandalled feet. The situation felt suddenly hopeless. Ava had vanished, just as Griff Fletcher had. They'd lost her.

Right in the middle of Via Frattini, Samia stopped dead. Ignoring the tuts of people forced to veer round her, she stood, fear twisting in her stomach. 'Ava's disappeared.' Her voice rose to a panicked wail. 'Why did we leave her there, all alone? What were we thinking?'

Reaching her, Frankie took her hand and pulled her into a shop doorway, out of the way of the surging crowds. 'Sam, keep the heid. We'll find her. She can't have been kidnapped or anything, not when she has left a trail for us.'

'She might have left on her own, but anything could have happened to her in the last half hour. We've no idea where she is. There are no more arrows!'

'Aye, true enough. It's like in that fairy story isn't it?

That wee guy Hansel must have been gutted when the birds ate his trail of breadcrumbs.' He wrinkled his nose. 'Not such a brilliant plan after all, pal.'

Samia wasn't sure if Frankie meant Ava's arrow idea or Hansel's breadcrumb trail, but his gruff voice and steady presence made her feel a little calmer. Miss Watson joined them, dabbing her flushed cheeks with a pristine white handkerchief.

'Come along, children. What are you doing, dawdling in a shop doorway?'

'Miss Watson, shouldn't we call the police?'

The woman physically recoiled, as if Samia had sworn at her. 'Certainly not. We just need to keep heading down this street until we find the next marker. Step lively.'

Nodding, Samia stepped back into the busy street, elbows jutting.

Right, girl. You're the star jammer in a roller derby bout and all these guys are trying to block you. You're going to send them flying. They're not going to know what's hit them.

For a few metres Samia made good progress, but her resolve was beginning to flag when finally, she spotted the arrow. It had been made from a discarded paper cup, torn into a rough arrow shape and precariously balanced on top of a bollard at the end of the Via Frattini.

The arrow pointed left, towards a narrow, cobbled street, its plaque proclaiming it as Via de Campio Marzio.

'This way!' Samia shouted. Miss Watson followed, her heels click-clacking. Frankie called Ava's name and a couple of women turned to stare, but for once, Samia didn't care what other people thought. She started shouting too.

'Ava! Ava!'

And as if she'd summoned up a ghostly apparition, a slight figure in jeans and faded purple t-shirt stepped out of a shop doorway right in front of her.

Samia blinked, hardly daring to believe. 'Ava!' Shoulders sagging with relief, she crumpled against a wall, tears nipping her eyelids. 'Ava, you're okay!'

Miss Watson had skidded to a halt too, and was attempting to regain her composure, fanning her face with her sunhat, breathing hard. She faced Ava, voice trembling. 'Why on earth didn't you follow instructions, child? We were all worried sick!'

'I wanted to find out where the person in the hoodie was going. I thought she might lead us to that... to Marlena Malcoeur. But my stupid ankle hurt too much. I've lost her.'

To Samia's astonishment, Ava started to cry, great heaving sobs. Embarrassed for her, Samia shuffled from foot to foot, trying not to look, while Miss Watson gave Ava an awkward pat on the back. It was Frankie who put his arm round the distraught girl's shoulder.

'There, there, hen. Let it oot. I always feel better after

a greet.' His tone was so comforting, that Samia felt her own stress levels dip a little. Gradually, Ava's crying stopped and Miss Watson passed her a tissue so she could clean the snot and tears from her face.

'I'm fine, honest. Sorry.' Ava leaned against a wall, face grey, eyes red-rimmed, clearly far from fine.

'That's aw that matters.' Frankie's smile revealed all his crooked teeth. 'We thought you'd been run oer by wan o those wee scooters—or maybe kidnapped by mad aliens.'

Miss Watson sighed. 'I feel quite discombulated. I need to take some deep, relaxing breaths... in through my nose and out through my mouth.'

After a few moments, she placed her sunhat firmly back on her head, her composure restored. 'Francis has made an excellent point. Nothing untoward has happened to you, Ava, and that is the main thing. Tell you what, children. We are only a few metres from the Pantheon, which we can explore later. But for now, let's go and have lunch, so that Ava can have a good rest, and we can read the next clue. Won't it be wonderful to discover where we are going next?'

It was only once she'd eaten her third slice of pizza with salami that Samia began to properly relax. The colour had returned to Ava's face, although her eyes were still puffy from the crying earlier, and she was tucking into the delicious gooey-cheese pizzas they were sharing.

The pizzeria was almost next door to the Pantheon, and Miss Watson insisted on telling them about the temple's history while they sat under a sunshade and ate.

'The inscription on the front of the Pantheon says *Marcus Agrippa built this*, but that isn't strictly true,' she finished. 'The building that we are looking at now was actually completed by Emperor Hadrian.'

'Ancient Fake News,' murmured Frankie.

'Ha, indeed, but it is the interior which makes this temple worth seeing, so we will have a look in a while, if Ava is feeling up to it.'

'I'm fine now, honestly. Sorry about earlier.' Ava looked down at the pavement, face flushing red.

Miss Watson's voice was surprisingly gentle. 'Ava, I know that when we first met I insisted that you must keep quiet about your story, but I think perhaps it would be helpful if Samia and Francis knew the whole truth. It would help them understand.'

Ava nodded, but for a long moment she didn't speak. Samia and Frankie waited as she picked up pizza crusts and threw them to the sparrows. Then she took a huge breath, and her words tumbled out in a rush.

'Griff Fletcher was my mum's younger brother. My dad left when I was a baby, so he was the closest thing I had to a dad.' A single tear dripped down her cheek and splashed onto the tablecloth. 'My Uncle Griff was the best. He took me skiing, sailing- once we even took a trip in a hot air balloon. He never forgot my birthday.'

I was devastated when Mum sat me down one evening and told me he'd disappeared and was presumed dead. I knew right away what must have happened. My uncle had told me he worked for MI6 and was involved in top secret missions. He'd sworn me to secrecy, and I'd been so proud, but also I never stopped worrying about his safety. When I heard he'd disappeared, I suspected one of his enemies had found out what he was doing and killed him. I was desperate to find out what had happened, but felt totally helpless. It was terrible, and I couldn't talk to anyone about it, not even Mum.'

Taking a big, gulping breath, she carried on with her story.

'When my teachers at school started going on about an essay competition to win a trip to Europe, at first I wasn't interested, cos I'm rubbish at essay writing, but then I figured a European trip would be a chance to visit some of the places Uncle Griff had been. So, without telling my school what I was doing, I submitted a video saying I wanted to win because my Uncle Griff had told me all about the wonderful cities of Europe. I said that he'd died very recently and I was really sad about it and wanted to go where he'd been, as a sort of tribute. And then, two weeks ago, Miss Watson visited. She explained who she was, and that she'd been a colleague and friend of my uncle. She told me that the trip was a cover, and she said she was sure my gut feeling had been right. My uncle's disappearance was no accident. Marlena Malcoeur, or one of her gang, killed him.'

'I think my exact words were that he had disappeared in suspicious circumstances.' Miss Watson patted Ava's hand. 'I can't be sure what has happened.'

'Not yet.' Ava's eyes glittered with loathing. 'But I'm going to find out, and when I do, I'm going to make sure they pay for what they've done.'

Miss Watson peered over her sunglasses. 'That's my job, my dear. Not yours. Perhaps we should relax a little while longer before we examine the new clue. I am going to have an *affogato*. Who else would like dessert?'

Samia ordered a *stracciatella* flavoured *gelato*, which turned out to be vanilla, with little bits of chocolate. It was yummy, but not quite as exotic as she'd hoped from the name.

'What are you enjoying most about our trip to Europe, Francis?' asked Miss Watson, as she poured hot coffee over her ice cream.

Frankie thought for a moment. 'The scran's no bad at aw. An findin the clues is a good laugh.' He paused. 'But the best bit's bein away from my maw for a wee while.'

Behind her dark glasses, Samia saw Miss Watson blink. 'Your mother? Is she unkind to you?'

'Och, no. My maw's sound. The best. But she's got MS an she needs a lot o lifting. The school have arranged respite carers for while I'm here an I'm hopin she'll be up for keepin them on when I get back.'

Samia and Ava stared at him. Frankie was so slight, he looked like a strong wind could blow him away. It was hard to imagine him lifting an adult. For his sake, Samia hoped his mum would keep the carers on when Frankie returned from Europe.

'I hope so too, Francis." Miss Watson patted the boy's hand. "Having such a big responsibility on your shoulders must be a terrible burden.'

Frankie shook his head. 'Naw, it's no like that. Like I said, my maw's sound. We have a good laugh.' He took a massive slurp of his lurid pink grattachecca, then swirled the crushed ice with his straw. 'Let's have a wee look at the clue, eh?'

11

PANIC IN THE PANTHEON

Miss Watson nodded, lifted her handbag and undid the clasp. Her expression of distaste as she tried to smooth out the chewing gum covered paper was so hilarious that Samia and Frankie started giggling, and even Ava managed a shaky smile.

On one side of the paper was a rough sketch of a carnival mask. Miss Watson's face brightened.

'Oh, that's a lovely surprise! Another Italian city, and this one's my favourite.'

Samia had read her *European Landmarks* book so often that she'd memorised some sentences, and at the sight of the mask, two lines from the book flashed through her head.

The Carnevale di Venezia is one of the most famous in the world. Thousands of tourists visit during carnival week to admire the masked parades in the city squares.

'We're going to Venice!' Samia felt her breath catch in her throat, and she couldn't say anything else, as she pictured the glorious images in *European Landmarks*: Piazza San Marco, the Grand Canal, the Rialto Bridge.

Maybe we'll have a trip in a gondola!

But then she had to refocus, because Miss Watson was reading out the clue, her voice hushed.

'All it says is: *Stolen twice, copied once.*' She sighed and spoke in an even quieter voice, not addressing them at all. 'Oh, Griff, you never stopped playing games. Did you have to make this one so hard?'

She's not wrong. It's too hard. I haven't a clue.

Samia felt her stomach tighten, and her muscles tense. She wanted so much to be able to tell the others what the clue meant, but she didn't know. It didn't matter how often she repeated the words *stolen twice, copied once—stolen twice, copied once—*she couldn't will them into sense.

Unexpectedly, Ava gave her a quick, awkward hug. 'Samia, it's okay. We'll work it out somehow, and even if we can't, it won't be your fault. You've been brilliant.' Then she threw her other arm round Frankie's shoulders and hugged him too. 'You too, Frankie. I know I've been acting like an eejit, but I was sworn to secrecy about my reasons for coming, so I thought it best just to pretend this trip was a bore.' She paused, and tears sprang in her eyes. 'But being here, it's made me feel closer to my Uncle Griff. It's like I'm literally following in his footsteps. It has been amazing. And I'm really glad you two are so good at solving the clues, cos they're pretty fiendish.'

'You've worked out the Métro passwords so far *and*

you got the skates/Keats clue,' Samia pointed out. 'It really has been a team effort. I just hope we can figure this new one out.'

Miss Watson stood up and smoothed the fabric of her pink dress.

'We will succeed. Of that, I have no doubts at all. But let us go now and experience the glorious interior of the Pantheon!'

As they walked between the temple's giant Egyptian granite columns, the light started to dim. Inside the massive round space, the only natural light came from a circular hole in the roof.

Miss Watson pointed upwards. 'The beam of sunlight coming through the oculus acts as a massive sundial.'

'Does the flair no get wet when it rains?' asked Frankie.

Miss Watson gestured at the richly patterned marble floor.

'Can you see the bronze disc in the centre? It has holes to allow rainwater to drain away. The whole building is an architectural marvel. The recesses around the centre originally housed statues of the Roman Emperors but are now tombs and chapels.'

Samia tore her gaze from the oculus and glanced around at the walls. A beam of light washed across one wall, splashed on the floor, glinted on an ornately decorated altar. The Pantheon was a magical, mystical place. But there was something here that wasn't right; as she stood in its centre, she felt a prickling sensation on her scalp.

Someone's watching us.

She tried to shake off the feeling of unease, and enjoy the beauty of her surroundings. But, as she walked around, she saw something move in a shadowy recess. Samia gasped, and clutched Frankie's arm.

'See, in that recess over there… I'm sure someone's hiding.'

Together, they took a few steps nearer, towards the roped-off area. Samia read the sign.

'*The tomb of King Umberto the First.* Nobody's allowed to enter this area. I was probably imagining things.'

Frankie pulled a spooky face. 'Maybe it was a zombie, risin from the grave? Or the Vampire King.'

But Samia wasn't in the mood for joking. The unsettling feeling of being watched had intensified here in the shadows. 'Cut it out, you eejit. There's nothing there. Let's go.'

Still laughing, Frankie glanced around to check nobody was looking, and vaulted the rope.

'Frankie, don't be daft!'

But she couldn't leave him there alone, so she stepped over the rope too, into the tomb of a long-dead Italian king.

Frankie had positioned himself behind the left-hand

pillar. As Samia stepped forward, he keeked round it, pulling another face. She shrieked, and the sound echoed eerily.

'Give over, Frankie,' she sighed, leaning against the pillar to slow her pounding heart. 'Can we get out of here, before we get caught by a security guard and get a massive telling off from Miss Watson?'

At that moment, the sunbeam slanting through the oculus shifted and sunlight shone into the recess. Frankie grabbed Samia's arm. 'Over there!' he hissed.

Spot-lit in the dazzling beam, a hooded figure crouched behind the other pillar.

A metal object glinted in their hand.

'Oh, jeez,' breathed Frankie. 'They've got a chib!'

Most of the person's face was covered by the hood, but Samia caught a glimpse of a scowl and long, black hair.

'It's the girl from the alley, I'm sure of it. Run!' As one, they jumped the rope barrier and ran across to the altar, where Miss Watson and Ava were taking photos. Heart racing, Samia told them what she and Frankie had just seen.

Miss Watson took immediate control. 'We need to leave right now, and make sure we shake this person off. Follow me!'

Outside the Pantheon, they were once again assailed by the intense heat and the din of traffic. Miss Watson led them through the crowd towards one of Rome's many hop on/hop off buses and stepped aboard.

'Go up to the top deck,' she ordered. 'Don't draw attention to yourselves.'

'Not exactly a speedy get-away car,' grumbled Ava, as she flung herself down beside Samia at the back of the open top deck. 'These things move at speed of slug.'

'Aye, but the lass in the hoodie doesn't have a clue where we've gone.' Frankie threw himself down in an empty seat. 'I just spotted her in the square—starin aboot with a face that would sour milk.' He waved his disposable camera in the air. 'I took a wee photie!'

Miss Watson sat down beside Frankie, bus tickets in her hand. 'Did you now? I do recall I instructed you not to draw attention to yourself.' She adjusted the brim of her sunhat so it shaded her face. 'Well, these buses are not my preferred mode of transport, but hopefully, we can enjoy our tour. This bus stops at the Termini Station, so no more walking for you today, Ava, I am sure you'll be relieved to hear.'

It was only when the bus swung out into traffic, blasting its horn, that some of the tension left Samia's body. Because down in the square, she could see the back of a short figure draped in an oversized grey hoodie. Strands of greasy black hair swung from side to side, as the girl's head swivelled, searching for her vanished prey.

Despite the fact that they saw the Roman Forum,

Vatican and Sistine Chapel without having to leave the bus, by the time they got on to the Euro Métro, they were all tired. Luckily, the password hadn't changed, because Ava didn't look as if she'd any energy left for cracking codes.

After all the pizza they'd consumed at lunchtime Miss Watson seemed to be working on the assumption that the children wouldn't be particularly hungry.

'Maybe you should have something light, like soup, and get to bed early? Ava looks exhausted.'

Ava shook her head, looking appalled at the prospect of soup. 'I'm shattered and sore, but also ravenous.'

'Aye, I could eat a scabby horse,' agreed Frankie.

Luckily, dinner was a massive and very filling dollop of (hopefully horse-meat-free) lasagne, bubbling with melted cheese. The lasagne was followed by a delicious dessert of vanilla panna cotta with caramelised orange.

They were so busy enjoying the meal that none of them spoke much, although they did spend a few minutes after dinner discussing the possible meaning of the latest clue.

Stolen twice. Copied once.

Something about *stolen twice* was ringing a distant bell in Samia's head. Had she read it somewhere? Perhaps the answer to this clue lay in the pages of her *European Landmarks* book. Yawning, she leaned her head against the train window.

'Good gracious, Samia's falling asleep.' Miss Watson laid down her napkin. 'It's definitely time for you children to get to bed. Tomorrow, we wake up in Venice!'

With her sore ankle, it made sense for Ava to take the bottom bunk again, and as soon as she was under the covers in the top bunk, Samia switched on the little reading light. She could hear Ava's slow, steady breathing and realised she must have fallen asleep immediately.

There were lots of facts about Venice, and Samia had read them all before. But this time she scanned the text, searching for the words *stolen* and *copied*. When she found them, her heart started beating faster. She closed the book, elation fizzing in her chest.

Tomorrow, we'll be in Venice. And I know where to look for the next clue!

But as she switched off the light, and huddled under the covers in the darkness, the excitement fizzled out and was replaced by fear. The image of the creepy, shadowed figure in the Pantheon kept flickering in her brain.

We must be closing in on the place Griff Fletcher hid the top-secret information, whatever it is, and these evil people seem determined to stalk our every move. If they're watching us when we find the intelligence, they're bound to try and stop us passing it to MI6.

A horrible thought gripped Samia by the throat, making it hard to breathe.

This train's taking us towards terrible danger.

12

VIOLENCE IN VENICE

Frankie was desperately keen to take a water taxi from Venice St Lucia station, but Miss Watson vetoed that plan.

'We'll go by water bus. It's much more economical.'

Frankie's lip curled at the sight of the crowded *vaporetto*. 'Och, the spies in the movies ALWAYS go into Venice by speed boat. They NEVER take the ruddy bus.'

But even though a water taxi would have been awesome, and the *vaporetto's* progress was slow in comparison, it was still incredibly exciting to head along the glittering green waters of the Grand Canal. Around their boat, barges chugged and water taxis zoomed. The banks of the canal were lined with ancient domed palaces and faded pink mansions with massive arched windows. A gondola glided sedately past, a couple kissing in the back, a gondolier steering the boat with a long pole.

'Venice is magical,' sighed Miss Watson. 'The most romantic city in the world.'

'They need to get a room.' Ava screwed up her face. 'Snogging in public. Gross.'

After about ten minutes, the *vaporetto* stopped by an elegant stone bridge. As Miss Watson ushered them off the boat, she explained where they were.

'This is the Rialto Bridge. It is a very expensive place to buy souvenirs, so keep your money safely in your pockets.'

Miss Watson led the way down a narrow street, past intriguing shops selling expensive leather bags, carnival masks and delicate glass ornaments.

'If we have time this afternoon, we must visit Murano, where Venetian glass is made!' she declared. 'So many wonders, so little time. If only we could work out the solution to the clue right now, we could enjoy the rest of our day.'

Samia chewed on her lip. After what had happened in Bern, she was reluctant to announce that she'd solved the clue, just in case she was wrong. She *so* hated being wrong. The prospect made her insides squirm. But she remembered what Ava had told her and it gave her the courage to speak.

'*Stolen twice. Copied once.* I think the clue might be St Mark's.'

They all turned to stare at her, and Miss Watson shook her head, 'No, dear. I'm sure the design of the basilica has been copied, but I don't think it would be possible to steal a whole cathedral.'

'No, I meant the next clue's *in* the cathedral. I checked

in my book last night.' Samia took a deep breath. 'There are four bronze horses on the balcony of St Mark's. But they are copies. The originals are inside the museum to keep them safe from the elements.' As she spoke, her conviction grew, and her voice got stronger. 'The bronze horses were stolen from the Hippodrome in Constantinople in 1204, during the Crusades, and taken to Venice. Then in 1797, they were stolen from Venice by Napoleon Bonaparte, who put them up on the Arc de Triomphe in Paris. France returned the horses to Venice in 1815. So—'

'They were stolen twice, and copied once.' Ava clapped her hands in delight. 'Brilliant work, Sam!'

As they walked into St Mark's Square, Samia gazed around, entranced. It was still fairly early in the day, and it wasn't too crowded, but the cafés were busy with customers sitting under parasols drinking espressos and cappuccinos. The square was surrounded by elegant arcades and huge buildings with massive, curved entrance ways and tiered rows of windows. The outside of the cathedral was magnificent, a froth of ornate stonework and shimmering mosaics above the portals. Beside her, Miss Watson was making hen-like clucking noises.

'Come along, children. The cathedral's about to open and the early bird avoids the worst of the queues.'

As they finally entered the basilica itself, Frankie

gasped. 'Jeez. Somebody's in the money.'

The interior of St Mark's cathedral glittered with gold. It was like stepping into Aladdin's cave. Exquisite ceiling mosaics, painted with real gold leaf, glimmered above them. Sunlight from stained glass windows shimmered on priceless sculptures and paintings.

Ava wrinkled her nose. 'Glitzy.'

'I'd have used the word glorious myself,' said Miss Watson. 'Sadly though, the Bible's *"Thou shalt not steal"* Commandment was conveniently ignored. A lot of this precious treasure was brought here after being stolen during the Crusades.'

Miss Watson waved the museum tickets she'd purchased at an attendant. They headed upstairs and went straight for the bronze horses. The animals were almost full-size, and incredibly life-like. Hooves raised, snorting, they eyed each other, as they thundered around an imaginary stadium, dragging an invisible chariot behind them.

'These are the originals,' explained Samia. 'The copies are outside on the balcony.'

Miss Watson nodded. 'Ava, you and Samia go out and inspect the copies. Frankie and I will have a good look at these. Do NOT draw attention to yourselves. The security guards are watching our every move.'

Frankie pulled a face. 'They'd have a brass neck moanin if we nicked any o this, when it's aw stolen property.'

The view of the square and the bell tower from the balcony was stunning. Samia and Ava took a moment to lean over the long expanse of stone railing, enjoying the little breeze and warm sunshine.

Ava pointed out the horses, standing in pairs at either end of the balcony, high on pedestals.

'I think the clue will be on the originals. I doubt Griff would have put a piece of paper out here, exposed to the wind and rain. And they're too high up for us to properly check without climbing. I don't think the security guards will be too chuffed if they spot us trying to get on the horses' backs.'

Samia nodded. 'Agreed. But we should have a quick look, just to be sure, while it's quiet. Bet this balcony will be swarming with tourists any moment. I'll check over this pair, you look at the other two.'

Samia had just started to check around the bottom of the first pedestal, when Ava swore loudly.

Yay! She's found the clue already!

But when Samia whirled round, she saw Ava, face pale and strained, walking along the balcony towards her. Just behind, a cloaked figure in a glittery carnival mask floated eerily. For a moment, Samia thought she was seeing a ghost, and blinked, hoping the apparition would dissolve into mist.

But the spooky creature didn't vanish, just kept moving slowly, red velvet cloak swishing on the tiles, piercing eyes staring through the slits in the mask.

As Ava reached Samia, the fear in the girl's eyes mirrored her own. 'Sam, stay totally still. They've got a knife.'

The masked figure stopped, only a couple of metres away. When they spoke, Samia jumped.

'This is no ordinary knife.'

Although muffled by the mask, Samia could tell the voice was female, English speaking, no particular accent.

The woman raised her left hand, and a bone-handled knife cut the air, its sharp blade glinting in the sunlight. 'This is an original 19th Century Spanish dagger. And it is as needle-sharp now as when it was forged.'

The cloaked figure took a step closer to Ava and Samia, who were trapped, their backs pressed against the horses' pedestal.

'Now, let us get straight to the point.' Jabbing the air with the dagger, the woman laughed at her own joke. 'For weeks, we have been checking the Métro, convinced someone would come to collect the data stolen by the traitor. We have been tailing you since London, and as we suspected, you are following the traitor's route. We presume this is merely a futile attempt to shake us off, and that you already know where our property is hidden, and may indeed have already found it. If you tell us what you know, we shall leave you alone. Our quarrel is not with children.' She gave another mirthless laugh.

'Our fight is with the weak governments of Europe, who refuse to acknowledge the superiority of the Ayran race.'

Samia's fists clenched. 'The Nazis lost. It's over, you idiot!'

Without warning, Ava launched herself forward, hands tearing at the stranger's mask. But the mask was firmly tied and didn't budge. As the woman jerked to the side, her cloak hood tumbled, revealing shoulder length fair hair, before she pulled the hood swiftly back over her head.

Again, Ava threw herself forward, trying desperately to pull off her mask.

'Get away from me, you little fool!' As the woman raised her hand again, Samia gasped in horror. The dagger blade flashed, slicing the sleeve of Ava's jacket. Panicked, Ava curled in a ball, trying to protect herself. Eyes glittering with fury, the masked stranger raised the knife once more.

'Woah! Leave her alone!'

Later, Samia couldn't imagine where she'd found the courage. Reaching out with both arms, she shoved the woman backwards, so hard her body smacked against the balcony railings and nearly toppled over the edge. The dagger fell and skittered across the marble floor. Samia leapt towards it, just as a large group of tourists came clattering onto the balcony, cameras clicking, exclaiming about the view, the mosaics, the gleaming white marble statues, the unexpected figure in the carnival mask.

'Look, Daddy. That lady's wearing a costume!'

'Oh, wonderful! May we take your photo?'

The masked woman stepped forward, sweeping the bottom of her cloak over the fallen dagger. She raised both hands and spoke to the man as if she were a tour guide, rather than an attempted murderer.

'*Naturalmente è possibile scattare una foto.* Of course, you may take a photograph. *Questa maschera è molto vecchia.* This mask is very old.'

The tourists' phones began snapping the scene, leaving Samia and Ava caught in the crowd. Samia opened her mouth, about to scream—*She's a psycho! She's got a knife!*

But Miss Watson had appeared on the balcony. Looking utterly unruffled, and ice-cool in her pale blue dress, she moved through the crowd until she was right next to the girls. 'Are you unhurt?' she asked in a low voice.

When they nodded, without saying another word, Miss Watson took Ava's arm. Pushing her way through the throng, she guided the girl towards the doorway, Samia scurrying behind them.

As they headed down the stairs and made their way out of St Mark's Basilica, Frankie fell into step with Samia.

'How's Ava's jaikit ripped? Did she have a square go with wan o the bad guys?'

Miss Watson's voice snapped like a trap. 'Less talking, more walking, Francis.'

It was only when they'd pushed their way through the heaving crowds in St Marks' Square, jinked past a massive pillar topped by a winged lion, and arrived at the bank of the Grand Canal, that Miss Watson spoke. Not to the children, but to a gondolier, standing in one of the bobbing boats tethered to the bank.

'*Quanto costo?*'

When the man replied, she gave a little shudder, but ushered the children on to the bobbing boat, and then got in herself. As the gondolier pushed off from the bank, she leaned forward and touched Ava's ripped jacket sleeve.

'Tell me exactly what happened.'

Between them, Samia and Ava managed to explain, while Miss Watson turned pale, and Frankie's eyes sparkled.

'Wish I'd been there. I would have chucked her right oer the rail. Splat!'

Miss Watson pursed her lips. 'This has not to happen again, do you hear me, children? You must come straight to me at the first sign of danger. What were you thinking of, Ava, trying to tackle an armed assailant?'

Ava's glare was mutinous. 'I was thinking *there's Marlena Malcoeur, the evil Nazi who killed my uncle. And I was thinking I'm going to make sure she rots in jail for the rest of her life.'*

'We can't be sure of her identity, Ava, when she was wearing a mask.'

'She had fair hair,' Samia broke in. 'Like the woman in the photo you showed us. I agree with Ava. I think it might have been Marlena Malcoeur.'

Miss Watson spoke in a louder voice, for the gondolier's benefit. 'Oh, look children! We are passing underneath the Bridge of Sighs. Its name comes from the tragic sighs of condemned prisoners who crossed on their way to be executed and caught their last glimpses of Venice through its small windows. Isn't that sad?'

She lowered her voice again. 'Or the masked assailant may be yet another member of the group. There do seem to be more members left than Griff had thought, which is worrying.'

Ava shrugged off her jacket, then trailed her fingers through the canal's dark-green, rippling water. 'I'm not worried. And I'm right, I know I am. That was Marlene Malcoeur. And I'm going to make the evil witch pay for what she did.'

13

ENEMIES EVERYWHERE

The gondolier didn't seem in any rush, and the trip along the canal would have been a delightful and relaxing experience, if Samia hadn't felt so on edge.

'We'll have to go back to St Mark's, won't we?' she said, annoyed to hear a tremor in her voice. 'Cos we didn't find the clue.'

An image of the creepy masked figure gliding towards her, dagger raised, flashed through her mind, and she blinked to try and erase it.

Frankie's grin stretched across his face. 'Aye, we did. I spotted it, an Miss Watson was able to reach it. Pure teamwork.'

The tight feeling in Samia's chest eased a little.

I won't have to go back onto that balcony, and risk running into Marlena Malcoeur. And I was right about the bronze horses, after all!

Miss Watson unclipped her handbag and drew out a tiny ball of paper.

'The clue was wedged into the collar of one of the horses. Well done, Samia! You did it again.'

Samia noticed Miss Watson's fingers tremble, almost imperceptibly, as she unravelled the paper. Was she remembering that Griff Fletcher had been the last person to touch that paper, as he scribbled the note and crushed it into a tiny ball?

Samia could imagine Griff glancing around, checking he wasn't being watched, as he stuffed the paper into its hiding place, and rushed out of the building. How had he felt, she wondered. Was he scared out of his wits, knowing he was being hunted down? Or had he been enjoying outwitting his enemies, playing cat and mouse, keeping one step ahead?

On one side of the paper, there was a rough drawing of a circular object. For a few moments, Miss Watson studied the sketch in silence.

'Griff was no artist, but I believe that *thing* is intended to represent Vienna's giant wheel, the *Prater*. So, our next destination, and possibly our last, is that beautiful capital city.'

Ava's head jerked up. 'Why do you think it's our last?'

'Hush, Ava. Moderate your voice. Our enemies appear to be everywhere.' Miss Watson pointed to a faded mansion on the canal banks. 'Look, children! The Palazzo Soranzo! Isn't it stunning!' Miss Watson kept her gaze on the building and lowered her voice to a whisper. 'I'm just keeping the timeframe in mind. There were only a few days between Griff's final phone call and all trace of him being lost. We have so far visited Paris, Bern, Rome and Venice and I feel that we are, literally, beginning to run out of time.' She paused, perhaps realising how difficult that realisation must be for Ava. 'I don't know for sure, dear.'

Frankie was looking thoughtful. 'Maybe Fletcher flew instead of takin the subway.'

Eyes still sad, Miss Watson shook her head. 'I doubt that would have speeded him up. Remember places like St Mark's Basilica and the Louvre have fairly short opening hours, so getting to two landmarks in one day in separate countries would probably not have been doable. We believe he took the Euro Métro, just as we are doing.'

Ava gulped. Her eyes were brimming with tears. 'Okay. I understand. Can we hear the clue, Miss Watson?'

Miss Watson turned the paper over. She whispered the clue, her words almost drowned by the clang of a church bell and the clamour of tourists from a parapet above them. Leaning closer, Samia read the scribbled words, hoping seeing them would help.

A different lizard

'Could it be another anagram?' she wondered. 'The letters of lizard in a different order?'

'What, like *DRAZIL* or *ZILDAR* or *RALZID*?'

'Shush, Frankie.' Ava gestured towards the gondolier, who was leaning forward, listening, probably trying

113

to work out what strange new language Frankie was speaking.

'We shall discuss this at another time.' Miss Watson popped the clue in her handbag and snapped it shut. 'I can't help feeling Griff Fletcher rather enjoyed thinking up these tricky clues!' She smiled and adjusted her sunhat. 'That man lived life to the fullest. Let us enjoy each moment too. Look around—is this not magical?'

Samia watched as the gondolier, smart in his striped polo-shirt and straw boater, used the long oar to push through the sun-splashed green waters of the canal. On either side, ornate palazzos rose dream-like from the water. Venice *was* a magical place and she was so glad she'd made the decision to come on this adventure.

I don't want it to end yet. Being followed by those people is scary, but visiting all these wonderful places is so exciting, and solving the clues is brilliant fun.

Samia was roused from her thoughts when another gondola almost crashed into theirs, and the two gondoliers started yelling and gesturing at each other. Other boats slowed down, seeming more than willing to join in the argument.

Frankie's eyes lit up. 'Aw man, an Italian rammy!'

The quarrel ended as quickly as it had begun, and their gondolier pushed off from the bank, still cursing.

When they got off the gondola they walked through some enchanting little alleys and over humpbacked bridges to a busy market square, Campo Santa Margherita. There, they sat on a bench in the shade of some trees and fed the sparrows on breadcrumbs while they ate panini filled with pink slices of ham and caramelised onions, washed down with fizzy lemonade.

Miss Watson flicked a crumb from her dress and stood up.

'It is getting rather crowded in central Venice now, and I have to confess to being a little anxious after the incident at St Mark's. I vote we get aboard a *vaporetto* and visit the island of Murano.'

Frankie held up his disposable camera. 'This is full. What am I meant to do wi it?'

Miss Watson explained that the photos would need to be developed. They found a suitable shop down a small alley and left Frankie's camera behind, while they set off in a waterbus across the lagoon to Murano.

It was fascinating to watch the glassmaker blowing a molten bubble into a shimmering sapphire-blue vase, and to look round the factory shop at all the colourful ornaments. Frankie picked one up, and put it down again quickly. 'I would have got wan o those wee glass birds for my maw, but man, the prices are steep.'

The journey back was unbearably stuffy and warm, despite a few open windows, and Samia was glad to get off the crowded boat. Even Miss Watson looked hot and bothered, and kept fanning her face with her sunhat.

'Let's find somewhere quiet to have a cool drink,' she suggested.

It was a lovely idea, but there seemed to be a complete dearth of quiet places in the centre of the city. In mid-afternoon, Venice was bedlam; crammed with sightseers from the cruise ships and tourist coaches.

After they failed to find a seat in yet another café, Miss Watson stopped to purchase bottled water from a stall.

'I think it might be time to say farewell to Venice,' she sighed, dabbing her face with a tissue dipped in ice-cold water. 'There's a fast express train from here to Vienna. It leaves just before four. If we get on that, we will be in Vienna by midnight and can stay in a hotel there. It will make a pleasant change to enjoy ensuite hotel facilities instead of the Euro Métro cabins.'

Frankie frowned. 'Aye, but what about my photies? I'm meant to collect them the day.'

Miss Watson clicked her tongue. 'I confess I had forgotten about those.' She paused. 'The sensible solution is that Ava and I go and collect our luggage, organise the train tickets and hopefully book a last-minute hotel. Samia, you shall go with Frankie to the photo shop and meet us at the station. It's a fifteen-minute walk from here.' She lowered her sunglasses so they could see the stern look in her eyes. 'Do *not* get lost.'

Frankie popped into the photo shop and came out complaining bitterly about the extortionate cost. 'I was robbed in there. Hope these pictures are quality or I'm going to be ragin.'

'We'd better hurry, or Miss Watson will be raging, and she's a whole lot scarier.'

The two children were hurrying towards the station when Samia noticed a woman with long auburn hair sitting at a café table sipping an espresso. Grabbing Frankie's sleeve, she pulled him into a shop doorway.

'Sam, we don't have time for shoppin,' Frankie complained. 'An this wan sells booze. I'm tee-total.'

'Listen! See that woman over there? The one with the red hair, sitting by herself under the blue umbrella? I think that's the woman who was following us in Bern. She keeps checking her watch and looking up and down the street. Maybe she's waiting for Marlena Malcoeur.' Samia felt a shiver run up her spine. 'Maybe the whole group's gathering.'

'Can we no just saunter past an give her a wee wave? What's she goin to do aboot it? This place is rammed.'

'Don't be an eejit, Frankie. She might have a gun in her handbag or something. We need to get past her, without her seeing, so she has nothing to report to Marlena. The last thing we need is the whole gang following us to Vienna.'

At that moment, a large group of sightseers streamed past, scuttling after their guide, who seemed intent on doing a tour of Venice as speedily as possible.

'Come on.' Frankie stepped out the doorway and positioned himself to the right of a large lady, keeping step with her as she hurried after the guide. Samia followed, trying to hide herself within a family group. But to her horror, just as they reached the café, the guide stopped to point out a little church on the other side of the street.

'The Church of San Simeone Profeta was founded way back in the tenth century.'

Cameras started flashing, and the gathered crowd were getting in people's way. An angry cyclist rang his bell, and Samia saw the auburn woman turn her head to look. Their eyes met.

'Run, Frankie!' Samia grabbed the boy's arm and together they raced through the narrow alley, ducking round the sightseers, into the next street and then up the steps of a canal bridge. As they rushed across, Samia's heart was pounding and her forehead beaded in sweat. Frankie's breath was ragged. He kept turning his head to check if they were being followed.

'I can't see her,' he gasped, as they headed into St Lucia station. 'I think we've lost her.'

Samia bit her lip, wishing she shared Frankie's easy confidence. She had a horrible feeling that just because they'd lost sight of the woman, it didn't mean she wasn't watching them. And it didn't mean she wouldn't turn up on the train.

WHERE ARE WE?

1. THE OFFICIAL LANGUAGE OF THIS COUNTRY IS GERMAN.

2. THIS COUNTRY IS THE BIRTHPLACE OF SOME OF THE WORLD'S MOST FAMOUS COMPOSERS, INCLUDING SCHUBERT AND MOZART.

3. THIS SMALL COUNTRY SHARES BORDERS WITH EIGHT OTHER COUNTRIES.

14

A DIFFERENT LIZARD

The train from Venice to Vienna was fast, and it was lovely to have a view from the window for a change. Samia leant against the glass and watched villages, castles, lakes and mountains whizz by. At dinner time, they ate creamy tomato gnocchi in the restaurant car. When they'd finished dessert, a slice of sticky chocolate torte, Miss Watson told them to go back to their seats, while she had "a moment's peace from all your chatter".

As they made their way back to their carriage, Frankie turned and grinned.

'Did yous clock Miss Watson checking the wine list? I reckon she's planning to order a wee brandy.'

Flinging himself into his seat, Frankie pulled the packet of photos from his jacket pocket.

'Let's have a gander at these.'

He started to pass them round, commenting on each rather fuzzy view of a famous European landmark, as if the other two hadn't been there too.

'That's the Eiffel Tower, which wasn't designed by Eiffel at aw but by two guys who worked for him. They must have been pure ragin. There's the Colosseum's Gate of Death, where they lugged oot the deid gladiators.'

Samia passed a photo to Ava. 'There's you, eating an ice cream bigger than your face.'

'Either these disposable cameras are totally duff, Frankie, or you are the worst photographer in the universe,' sighed Ava.

'Oh, yikes. Look. There's the old woman!' gasped Samia. 'See her purple hair? Behind me on that bridge in Paris.'

She held up the photograph, of herself grinning cheesily on the Pont Neuf. In the background, Frankie had captured the elderly woman, swathed in a tartan cape, an umbrella in her hand.

Ava spread some of the photos out on the table, scanned them quickly, then snatched one up.

'Sam... is that the red-haired woman who creeped us out in Bern?'

The photo, taken on the Euro Métro to Bern, had Samia in the foreground, pulling a silly face. But the auburn-haired woman in the background, surrounded by a heap of shopping bags, a phone in her left hand, was definitely the same lady who had questioned them in Bern, and who she'd just seen in the Venice café.

'Ha! I've got aw the bad guys!' Frankie's voice was triumphant. 'Check it out, there's the other yin an aw!'

He threw the last photo down on the table.

It was the one he'd taken from the top deck of the bus in Rome, of a young woman with straggly black hair, dressed in an oversized hoodie, her head turned to the right, searching. A battered rucksack dangled from her left hand.

'What's all this about?'

At the sound of Miss Watson's voice, they all jumped like startled hares. They'd been so engrossed in the photos they had completely missed her arrival. Miss Watson sat down, and Frankie slid the photos across the table.

'I've nabbed the whole gang,' he crowed, and started gathering up his pictures. Miss Watson put her hand over the pile.

'I'll be needing those, Francis,' she said firmly.

Frankie rolled his eyes, but handed the photographs over without complaint. Then he lifted his backpack from the floor and took out a pack of cards.

'Who fancies a game o Twist?'

They played cards for a couple of hours, until Miss Watson said they should stop and have a sleep, or they'd be "fit for nothing" by the time they arrived in Vienna.

But Samia found that sleep was harder to come by sitting upright in a train seat than tucked up in a cabin bed. As the train shot across Northern Italy and into Austria, travelling over viaducts with awe-inspiring views of beautiful valleys and rolling hills, and through long tunnels cut through the mountains' rock, she gazed, bleary-eyed, out of the window. Daylight was fading, and as the clouds gathered on the mountain tops, it started to rain, droplets streaming across the glass.

As darkness fell, worries began to flap, scary as vampire bats, in Samia's head.

Leaning her head against the backrest, she closed her eyes, and took some deep, slow breaths.

The red-haired woman didn't get on board this train– I'm sure of it. Frankie and I kept looking behind us to check that she wasn't following us. But maybe she figured she doesn't have to chase us because the gang has already worked out that we are travelling to Vienna next. They probably expect us to catch the Euro Métro tonight, because that's what we've done up until now. So, we're safe here on this train, for the moment. And they've no idea that we are following hidden clues. All we have to do is keep one step ahead, and keep going until we find the information.

She was drifting off to sleep, soothed by the rhythm of the train, but then another worry swooped into her brain and her eyes snapped open.

But we aren't one step ahead, are we? We're foundering. Without the solution to the clue, Vienna's a dead end.

She finally dozed off with the words *A different lizard…* rattling in her head.

Vienna's fancy main station, *Wien Hauptbahnhof*, was

enormous, bright and glossy, with acres of glistening glass and shiny tiled floors. Without any fuss, Miss Watson ushered them into a taxi, and directed the driver to their hotel. Just after midnight, Samia crawled into a comfortable twin bed and fell instantly asleep, like a wild animal hit by a tranquiliser dart.

They met, as arranged, for breakfast at nine thirty. Frankie went up to the buffet counter and came back with a plate piled high with delicious looking pastries. He sat down, a satisfied grin on his face. 'I'm goin to get wired into this lot. When I get hame, it'll be back to stale cornflakes at the school's breakfast club.'

Miss Watson entered the dining room and swanned over to their table, looking very chic in a white blouse and striped navy skirt. After she'd sipped a black coffee, she focused her gaze on the children, crimson lips pursed in disapproval.

'Heavens, you're all looking rather dishevelled. I hope you showered, at least.'

Samia felt heat burn her neck, as she glanced down at her crumpled t-shirt and unwashed jeans. In comparison to the as-always immaculate Miss Watson she supposed they did look scruffy. The mosquito bite on Frankie's cheek was red and swollen and Ava's magenta hair was hanging in damp rats' tails, uncombed after her morning shower.

But Frankie just grinned, puffed out his chest and ran

nail-bitten fingers through his baby-hedgehog spiked hair. 'I'm grand, Miss Watson. Ta for askin.'

Ava too ignored the comment completely. Biting into one of Frankie's pastries, she spoke with her mouth full. 'Any clues about the clue, guys?'

Frankie shook his head. 'Naw. Maybe if we go for a wee dauner roon the toon we'll spot a statue o a gecko. Or maybe the zoo's got wan o those freaky Komodo dragons?'

'A walk around the city appears to be as good a plan as any.' Miss Watson stood up, swinging her handbag. 'Let's go. Francis, put those pastries down. DO NOT put that apple strudel in your pocket!'

'No bother.' Grinning, Frankie shoved the apple strudel in his mouth and popped a cinnamon bun in his jacket pocket.

Miss Watson gave a resigned sigh. 'Perhaps a smidgeon less sticky. Right children, let's go and find *a different lizard*.'

Outside the hotel, trams clattered noisily along the wide streets. The children followed Miss Watson as she marched across the road, seemingly oblivious to the traffic, and walked through tall black wrought iron gates.

'This is the *Volksgarten*, or people's garden. It's famous for its beautiful rose bushes. Can you see those two domed buildings in the distance? The one on the left is Vienna's Museum of Fine Arts and the other is the Natural History Museum.'

Frankie scratched at his mosquito bite, his eyes thoughtful. 'The Natural History Museum? They'll have stuffed animals... mammals, an amphibians, an reptiles... lizards maybe?'

'Oh, good thinking, Francis! There are bound to be lizards in there!' Miss Watson's face brightened, and she spun in a circle, her striped skirt swirling. 'Breathe in the glorious scent of the roses, children!'

It dawned on Samia that Miss Watson too had been worried that Vienna was going to be a dead end. If it had been up to Samia, they'd have headed straight for the Natural History Museum, but Miss Watson seemed determined to stop and sniff every one of the million rose bushes in the *Volksgarten*. The formal layout of the garden, with its plane trees, Narnian lamp posts and stacks of green metal chairs, reminded Samia of the Tuileries Garden in Paris, and it gave her a little kick that she was now so well-travelled that she could compare parks in Europe's capital cities.

It was almost an hour later that they climbed the stone steps leading to Vienna's massive Natural History Museum. Inside was as grand as the exterior, with a magnificent domed ceiling and marble floor. The entrance hall led to a mezzanine level, and rooms full of glass cases, crammed with rocks and fossils.

'Reptiles are on the first flair,' said Frankie, bouncing with enthusiasm. 'Come on!'

The reptiles were in rooms 27 and 28, and there were lots of them: leatherback turtles, massive anacondas, rattlesnakes, caimans, crocodiles, a Komodo dragon, an extinct sub-species of tortoise. Plus chameleons, monitor lizards and every other sort of lizard, all displayed in tidy rows.

Ava ran a hand through her tangled hair. '*A different lizard.* Which of these lizards is any weirder than the rest? Answer: *they're all freaks.* I guess we'll have to check underneath all those glass cases.'

Samia grimaced. 'Hope your Uncle Griff hasn't used chewing gum again to keep the clue in place.'

'Aye, that was mingin',' agreed Frankie.

Ava stood in front of the nearest exhibit, and read the label aloud in a deeply sarcastic tone. '*The bridge lizard from New Zealand is known as a "living fossil". It differs little from its ancestors over 200 million years ago.*' Oh, that's absolutely fascinating—*not.*'

'So, the bridge lizard has been around since the time of the dinosaurs,' Samia mused. 'That's different, surely?'

Frankie's eyes widened. His hand flew to his mouth. 'Aw, no,' he groaned.

Samia whipped round, fear making her pulse race. Her thoughts flew to the spooky, cloaked figure in the Pantheon, the masked maniac on the balcony, both wielding knives. *Has he spotted one of the gang? Are they here, poised to attack?*

15

A VILLAIN IN VIENNA

Swearing loudly, Frankie banged his fist against his forehead. 'I'm a total numpty!'

'Tell us news, Frankie,' drawled Ava.

'Well, I've surpassed myself this time. The answer to the clue's *so* obvious.'

Miss Watson tapped her foot impatiently on the marble floor. 'Please feel free to share, Francis.'

'We're on the wrang flair o the museum. In Latin, '*different lizard*' is *Allosaurus*... the clue's on a ruddy dinosaur, no on wan o these guys.'

'Oh, excellent detective work!' Miss Watson's smile made her eyes twinkle. 'The dinosaur displays are on the mezzanine level. Let's go!'

Room 10 was a lot busier than the other rooms, noisy with the excited yells of small children. A massive skeleton of a *Diplodocus* spanned the length of the room, and above them hung a *Pteranodon*, frozen mid-flight. As Samia looked around, one of the models started to move.

'Aw, cool,' Frankie murmured. 'An animatronic

Allosaurus. That's oor man.'

The *Allosaurus* was surrounded by a group of kids from a nursery school outing, all running around, screaming with pretend terror, every time the dinosaur roared and snapped its huge jaws, while their teacher stared out of the window, a *kill me now* expression on her face.

'How are we goin to get past that squad o weans?' moaned Frankie.

Ava winked. 'I'll distract them for a second while you have a quick look. The most likely hiding place is under the feet. Good luck and try not to get eaten. Oh, before we start- Frankie, how do you say *jumped* in German?'

Casually, the three children walked over to the *Allosaurus* display, while Miss Watson feigned interest in a plaster model of an *Iguanodon*.

They were right behind the kindergarten group when Ava yelled at the top of her voice.

'Oh no! My pet mouse just jumped out of my pocket! *Meine maus ist gesprungen!*'

Wide-eyed, the nursery children turned to stare at Ava, who started to gesture frantically towards a huge glass case displaying fossilised dinosaur eggs.

'Quick, catch it! *Meine maus!*'

Squealing, the toddlers started running round the case, followed by their frazzled teacher. The poor woman's mouth was open, and presumably she was yelling at the kids to stop, but she couldn't make herself heard over the screeching of her out-of-control charges and the roaring of the animatronic *Allosaurus*.

Seizing the moment, Frankie reached under the *Allosaurus* model's clawed feet, while Samia felt around the base of the display stand.

There's nothing here. Frankie's got it wrong.

Stepping backwards, hope fizzling out, Samia was almost clobbered by the dinosaur's jaw, as it opened its mouth and roared again.

Samia blinked. She went very still, watching and waiting impatiently as the *Allosaurus* swung its massive head. As its jaws widened, she held her breath.

I DID see it. The clue's in its flipping mouth.

A tiny ball of blue paper was skewered on to one of the dinosaur's needle-sharp teeth. As the *Allosaurus* swung its thrashing tail and clawed at the air, Samia jumped, and stuck her hand in the creature's gaping jaws. As her fingers fumbled for the paper, she fell backwards, just as its mouth clamped shut.

'*Bitte nicht berühren!*' A security guard leapt from his chair, cap askew, face flushed purple with annoyance. He barged towards Samia, just as one of the feral pack of small children tripped, fell across the guard's path, and lay sprawled on the marble floor, kicking its legs and shrieking like a tiny banshee.

The teacher reacted with fury, as if she believed the

guard had knocked the kid over on purpose. While they were yelling at one another, the nursery kids swarmed over to the large central display area, heading for the *Diplodocus* skeleton, which Samia had to admit, did make a tempting climbing frame.

'I've got the clue,' she hissed to Frankie. 'Let's get out of here before we get kicked out.'

They headed for the entrance, gesturing at Miss Watson and Ava to follow. But as they made their way down the front steps, Samia froze. Her heart started banging against her ribs.

'Look over there. Walking away from the Museum of Fine Arts,' she hissed. 'It's the old woman from Paris.'

There was no mistaking that curly violet hair, or that distinctive tartan cape.

Hiding behind one of the immaculately manicured hedges, they watched the woman cross the concourse, and walk up the steps of the Natural History Museum.

Miss Watson turned to the children. 'She's clearly searching for us, so let's put some distance between us. As we're in Vienna, we really ought to visit one of their gorgeous cafés, despite Francis having gorged himself at breakfast.'

Frankie patted his stomach. 'No worries, hen. I've loads mair room in here.'

The café was very posh, with velvet drapes at the enormous windows, glittering chandeliers and polished mahogany tables, and Samia felt a little intimidated when she was presented with a menu by a rather stern waiter. But Frankie ordered for them, in fluent German: hot chocolate sweetened with vanilla and topped with cinnamon-powdered cream and a slice of glossy *sachertorte*, an Austrian chocolate cake with apricot jam.

Ava suggested they look at the clue, but Miss Watson seemed a little nervous and said they should wait. Every time the bell rang to signal the arrival of more café customers, she jumped and twisted round to check out the new arrivals.

'I've had an excellent idea. I think you children would enjoy a visit to the Prater Park. We can go for a ride on the Riesenrad, Vienna's giant Ferris wheel. It's further away from the museum area, which I think might be wise.'

With her stomach sloshing with hot chocolate, the thought of going on a fairground ride wasn't terribly appealing, but Samia could see Miss Watson was anxious to move on, so she didn't say anything, and both Ava and Frankie seemed keen.

'I've read about that theme park!' Ava was already tugging on her jacket. 'There's a space flight ride and a ghost train too. It'll be fun, and a nice change from churches and museums and art galleries.'

Frankie nodded in agreement. 'Aye. I'm goin to keel oer wi boredom if I have to look at wan mair picture o deid folk.'

As they left the café, Miss Watson scanned the street and then began to move at an almost jogging pace.

'It's like she's on one of those moving walkways you get at the airport,' Ava hissed as they scuttled after her. What's her flaming hurry?'

'She's worried that old wummin's comin after us wi a chib.'

At sixty-five metres tall, the Ferris wheel towered over the trees in the park. It was only when they'd climbed into one of the brightly painted red wagons and it had swung into the air, that Samia finally felt she could breathe freely. No enemies could reach them here. Miss Watson was clearly thinking the same thing, because as the Ferris wheel climbed higher, she opened her handbag, and unfolded the tiny ball of paper which Samia had handed over earlier.

Miss Watson turned the paper, then almost immediately, turned it again, a frown etching grooves on her face. Sighing, she raised her head skyward.

'For heaven's sake, Griff. This is useless.'

'Can I see?' asked Samia.

Shrugging, Miss Watson handed the clue to Samia. 'Good luck with this one.'

Samia stared at the paper, turned it over and gulped. One side was completely blank. There was no writing on the other side, other than a single word in the speech bubble above a hastily drawn stick figure. The word was so tiny it was almost unintelligible. But Samia had excellent eyesight, and she was totally determined to try.

'S-N-O... Frankie, is that next letter an *M* or a *V*?

Frankie pulled a face. 'Or a *W*? No idea. Ava, what do you think?'

Ava took the paper. As she looked at the drawing, a smile spread across her face. 'I know who that's meant to be! Uncle Griff and I used to draw and write comics together. See the quiff on the stick man's head? That's how Uncle Griff drew Tintin.'

Frankie scratched his head, a baffled expression on his face, but Samia recognised the name immediately. 'Oh, brilliant. I get it now!' She felt a surge of happiness, enjoying that they were working as a team. 'You were right, Frankie. It's a *W*. The word in the speech bubble is *SNOWY*—Tintin's dog in the comic strips. But how does Tintin help lead us to our next city?'

'We're heading for Brussels.' Miss Watson's shoulders straightened, and a smile flickered on her lips. 'There's a large Tintin shop in the city centre. I expect Griff has left the evidence with someone in the shop.' She glanced at her watch. 'It's only midday. We shall catch the Euro Métro to Brussels later this afternoon and will be there in plenty of time for the shop opening in the morning.' Gesturing out of the window, she *tsked*, as if the children had been remiss in not focussing on the views. 'Now, let us enjoy this fabulous panoramic view of Vienna from the top of this magnificent Ferris wheel. You're far too young to be familiar with the films, but this wheel appears in *The Third Man*, a very famous spy film, and it features in one of the old James Bond movies, so it is the perfect setting for spies like us!'

Spies like us… Can school kids really be spies?

It was an awesome thought.

The prospect of a successful end to her mission in Brussels seemed to have made Miss Watson almost giddy with anticipation. Even after they'd got off the wheel, she encouraged the children to go on some of the other rides in the amusement park, until Frankie, who'd scoffed the cinnamon bun in his pocket, along with the hot chocolate and massive slice of *sachertorte* at the café, came off the rollercoaster complaining of feeling sick. After they'd gone for a peaceful walk along the *Prater's* chestnut tree-lined boulevard, he'd recovered enough to buy a *Kasekrainer*, a cheese-filled sausage in a long roll with mustard and ketchup, at one of the *Würstelstands* in the park. Ava and Samia choose *Bratwurst*, a lightly spiced fried sausage, but Miss Watson turned up her nose at all of the available options.

Samia was still wiping grease from her chin when Miss Watson declared it was time to move on. Marching them out of the park, she led them to where a long line of pretty carriages stood, the horses pawing the ground impatiently, swatting flies with their long tails.

'Let us get aboard a more sedate means of transport and take in some of Vienna's magnificent buildings.'

Once aboard the carriage, Samia sat back on the padded bench and enjoyed the cool breeze, as the handsome chestnut horses clip-clopped through the narrow, cobbled streets of the old part of the city. As she gazed at the beautiful buildings, decorative and snowy-white as iced wedding cakes, her imagination took flight, and for a few glorious moments she was a fabulously rich Austrian princess in a glittering diamond necklace and crimson velvet gown, being transported by carriage to the Royal Opera House.

Or maybe I'll tell the coachman to take me to a Chinese restaurant for a five-course dinner, because I don't really fancy having to sit through an opera.

Frankie nudged her in the ribs. 'This is pure magic. I feel like Cinder-bogging-ella on the way to the baw.'

'Does that make Sam and me your ugly sisters?' laughed Ava.

'Aye. An Miss Watson's my pure evil step-maw.'

Miss Watson peered over the top of her sunglasses. '*Heaven forfend!* Being a stepmother is a dreadful fate which I intend to avoid like the plague.'

Samia glanced at Ava, and wondered if Miss Watson would have considered the role of step-aunt. It seemed terribly sad that Griff Fletcher's disappearance had ruined any chance of that ever happening, though maybe

Ava would have been less than thrilled by the prospect.

Finally, the carriage drew to a halt and they got out, and said goodbye to the horses while Miss Watson paid the bill. After collecting their luggage from the hotel, Miss Watson led them through the streets to a busy square.

'Follow me. We're heading for that blue U sign. *Stephansplatz* is the main station for the Vienna U-Bahn, or underground.' She glanced quickly at her phone, 'Oh dear, how terribly inconvenient. They've changed the password again. Looks like they're attempting to ramp up security. Ava, can you work this out? How does one create a password from this string of random numbers: 71, 32, 62, 41, 82, 43, 62?

'Oh, this one is quite cool. It's a phone cipher, so I'll need to look at your phone keypad to work it out.'

As they headed down the escalator, Samia felt elated.

We're getting back on the Euro Métro! We're heading to Brussels!

The others were in front of her, and she glanced behind, hoping for a final view of beautiful Vienna before it vanished from sight. A wave of dread swamped her and she gasped, struggling to breathe.

There, hovering at the top of the stairway, was the red-haired woman in her pink puffer jacket.

16

A DEVIL IN DISGUISE

Vienna's Euro Métro entrance was hidden deep underground, behind an unmarked door at the end of a long, featureless passageway. There was no one else waiting on the platform, but Samia was taut with nerves, jumping at every sound.

It feels like everywhere we go, one of those evil women appears. We're never going to escape. They're just waiting until we find the info and then they'll all gang up, and pounce.

Several times, she opened her mouth to tell the others, but saying it aloud would make it real, and their current situation, trapped deep underground on a deserted subway platform, was the stuff of horror movies. So, she tried to persuade herself that she'd been mistaken, or hallucinating. After all, she *was* shattered—so tired her eyes stung and her brain felt fuzzy.

When she heard the rumble of the train, and saw the eerie glow of its lights, she felt a little of the tension melt. The woman hadn't appeared. They were still the only people on the platform… just a few more seconds and they'd be safely on the train.

As the doors swished open and they stepped aboard the brightly-lit carriage, she breathed in the comfortingly familiar vanilla scent, and her shoulders sagged with relief. But before she sat down, she did a quick scan of the other passengers: a florid-faced middle-aged man, snoozing after his liquid-lunch, a sharp-suited businesswoman with a smart leather briefcase, her manicured fingers flying as she typed on her laptop, and a youngish lady with curly brown hair, talking loudly on her phone in Italian.

There was no sign of the red-haired woman.

Get a grip, girl. She couldn't possibly have got on the train before us. We've dodged her, again.

When dinner arrived, Samia felt so exhausted that she struggled to eat, although the *Kasespatzle*, cheese-covered egg noodles topped with crispy onions and chives, was delicious.

'Yum. Austrian macaroni cheese.' Ava shovelled another forkful in her mouth. 'You okay, Sam? You're a bit quiet.'

'Aye, Sam, what's up?' asked Frankie, concern in his kind eyes.

I have to tell them… just in case.

'On the escalator… I thought I glimpsed the red-haired woman standing at the top. But I might have been wrong… I'm dead tired and I might have imagined it.'

Quickly, Ava glanced around at the other passengers.

'What was she wearing?'

'Same as in Bern. Pink jacket, pale blue jeans... black high-heeled boots. She's not here. I've already checked.'

'Exactly the same outfit? Odd.' Ava chewed on her lip, her eyes thoughtful. 'And high-heeled boots are a weird choice of footwear for sightseeing... why would she wear those? Unless...' Her hand shot out, and she grabbed Miss Watson's sleeve. 'Miss, can I have another look at Frankie's photos?'

'Yes, of course you may, but I insist we finish our meal first, or we will all end up with indigestion.'

When the waiter had removed their plates, Miss Watson finally took the packet out of her bag, and slowly and carefully, Ava arranged three photos in a row. For a long moment she stared at them in silence, elbows on the table, hands supporting her chin, deep in thought.

When she finally spoke, her voice was so quiet Samia struggled to hear her.

'We've been really, really stupid. There aren't lots of people following us. These three women... *they're the same person*. They're all Marlene Malcoeur in disguise.'

Frankie screwed up his face. 'Ava, you're talking mince, hen. They're nothin like each other.' He jabbed a finger at the photo in the centre. 'That yin's a wee old wummin for starters.'

'Is she really? Or is she in disguise?' Ava spoke louder now, with more conviction. 'Look, her hairstyle is old-ladyish and she's wearing thick glasses and her back's bent, but her skin isn't really wrinkly, is it? And look at that! She's holding the umbrella in her left hand. Now look at the red-haired woman's phone… and hoodie girl's bag. They're all left-handed. Isn't that a weird coincidence?'

Samia's hand flew to her mouth. 'And so's Marlene Malcoeur. She was holding the dagger in her left hand!'

Ava nodded. 'If the old woman wasn't bent over, and the red-haired woman wasn't wearing high-heeled boots, I bet they'd be about the same height as the girl in the hoodie. And see the mole on hoodie girl's cheek? I'm sure the red-haired woman has the same mole, though it's covered by make-up. Can you see? It's a shame Frankie's photography skills are so rubbish. I can't see the old lady clearly enough to check out her moles.'

'Marlena Malcoeur has a mole on her cheek. It's visible in the mugshot I showed you.' Miss Watson let out a long breath. 'Well, well, well.'

She picked up the photos and examined them in silence, then laid them back down on the table. 'It's difficult to accept that I have been fooled by Marlena but have to admit that she is an exceptionally cunning opponent.'

Lifting one hand, she gave Ava a small salute.

'Well done, Ava, excellent work.'

Samia waited for her stomach to twist with envy, but

it didn't happen. She didn't feel envious of Ava's success, just proud of her friend. Ava's smile made her face light up, and under the table, Samia squeezed her hand.

Frankie whistled. 'So, we've been thinkin there's a whole gang, an it's aw the same wummin?'

'A very deliberate strategy by Marlena.' Miss Watson sighed. There was a dazed look in her eyes, as if she was still struggling to believe she'd been outfoxed by her deadly enemy. 'She has been attempting to convince MI6 that she is the leader of a network of neo-Nazis. But it seems that, since Griff's efforts and her brother's demise, she has been working entirely alone. If MI6 can put Marlena in jail, we will rid Europe of a dangerous lone wolf.'

Samia leaned her elbows on the table, and buried her head in her hands, trying to untangle her knotted thoughts.

If Ava's right, and we're possibly only dealing with one enemy now that Gabrielle has killed Marlena's brother, that's got to be better than several, hasn't it? But Marlena's clearly super-cunning and we know she's armed and dangerous. We're still in terrible danger. Could she somehow have sneaked on to this train? She must have fake identity papers and she is certainly smart enough to work out the new passcode.

It was an extremely unsettling thought, particularly now that she was aware of Marlena's ability to disguise her appearance. She sat up, and glanced anxiously around the carriage.

Could she be that lady at the back of the carriage, the one who keeps chatting loudly on her phone? Or the blonde woman with the leather briefcase? But that doesn't make sense. It can't be either of those people. If the red-haired woman on the escalator was Marlena Malcoeur, she didn't have a moment to get into another disguise before she got on this train... did she??

'Sam, are you okay?' Ava put a comforting arm around her shoulders, and kept it there, until Samia raised her head.

'Yeah, I'm fine. Honest.'

'You are clearly not fine.' Miss Watson clicked her tongue impatiently. 'You look dreadful. Totally washed out. Perhaps we should cancel dessert.'

Frankie groaned in horror. 'Tell me you're kiddin?'

'I agree Sam needs to have an early night, but no way should we cancel dessert.' Ava withdrew her hand from Samia's shoulder and crossed her arms. Her voice was firm, daring Miss Watson to argue. 'Can we all focus for two minutes on the Marlena Malcoeur situation? I need to get what's going on clear in my head. If the stuff that Griff downloaded from Marlena's computer isn't about the whereabouts of all the other members of their organisation, because there aren't any other members left standing, then what's it about? Why is she so desperate to retrieve it and why are you... *we*... going to all this trouble to find it first?'

Miss Watson nodded. 'An excellent question. And the answer is that we want to find the intelligence because we are fairly sure that Griff discovered a target list, which includes details of an imminent plot to destroy an important European landmark. Marlena's group has been making vague threats for years. The most famous buildings and monuments are well-guarded, as we have discovered while trying to retrieve the clues, and if Marlena intends to destroy one of them in the very near future, and to escape from the scene afterwards, she will need to have planned her every move in minute detail.'

Miss Watson fell silent, as the waiter had arrived with their dessert, an apricot cake with whipped cream, so delicious that Samia ate every spoonful, despite her exhaustion.

As soon as they'd finished, Miss Watson stood up.

'You children *all* look worn out, and I insist that you have an early bed. This train passes through Germany on its way to Brussels. It is likely to stop in Munich during the night. As I've stated previously, use the toilet facilities before you go to bed, and then stay in your cabins and do not leave them until morning. Goodnight, children. Hopefully, our adventure will come to a successful conclusion tomorrow. And Samia, please try and relax. As I've said before, the risk to you children is minimal.'

'Tell that to my jacket,' muttered Ava, as they walked towards the sleeper carriage. 'I'm lucky not to be scarred for life. Minimal risk, my butt.'

It felt good to be back in the tiny cabin. The girls brushed their teeth and climbed into their bunks. As Samia switched off her light and snuggled under the cosy duvet, Ava spoke, her tone serious.

'It'll sound weird, because I was just moaning about being attacked by a mad Nazi, but I'm really glad I came along on this trip. My original plan was to avenge my uncle, and I still want to do that, though I haven't a clue how. Also, I *really* want to find the target list Uncle Griff hid before he was murdered. But meeting you and Frankie has been so good.' She paused, and when she spoke again her voice sounded choked. 'I don't have any friends at my school. It didn't bother me... I thought I was a loner, I guess, and was okay with that. But we three have each other's backs, and it's kind of great. If Miss Watson's right, and this adventure does end tomorrow, I'd love to stay in touch.'

A warm feeling flowed through Samia, and she smiled in the darkness.

'That would be brill, and I know Frankie would be up for it. We could all meet up in Glasgow, as it's kind of in the middle, and it would be easiest for Frankie.' Samia pulled the covers over her head, muffling her voice. 'But I've got an odd feeling that us finding out which landmark Marlene's planning to destroy next won't be the end of this story.'

During the night, Samia woke to the squeak of brakes, as the train pulled into a station. Twitching her tiny curtain aside, she saw a metal plaque on the tiled wall, similar to the one in Glasgow.

München Hauptbahnhof

After the doors swished open, and then almost immediately closed, the train remained stationary for a few minutes. The loud beep, echoing in the night's silence, was interrupted by an electronic announcement.

'This train is ready to leave. Please mind the doors. Next station, Brussels Central.

As the train built up speed, Samia became aware of small sounds outside in the corridor. The sounds got louder, more insistent, like squirrels scrabbling in the attic, and then suddenly stopped.

It seemed only moments later that Ava was shaking her arm, announcing that they'd slept in and were meant to have met Miss Watson for breakfast five minutes ago.

Samia threw on some clothes, her last clean t-shirt— the vintage *Killers* one Shanaz had bought her for her last birthday—and a pair of black joggers, a bit tight around the waist. As she scraped a comb through her tangled dark hair, the girl in the mirror stared back, mouth firm, defiant, ready for anything.

But she wasn't ready for the shock that awaited the

girls when they left the cabin and knocked on Frankie's door. As the door swung open, Samia gasped. The contents of Frankie's battered rucksack were strewn across the floor: a guddle of dirty clothes, his toothbrush and the fancy toiletries he'd nicked for his mum from the hotel in Vienna. As Samia stepped into the cabin, she saw that the duvets on both bunks had been tugged right back and hung from the ends like puffy ghosts. A pillow had been tossed on the ground and a dirty footprint stamped on the snowy-white cotton.

Someone's been in here, pulling the place apart, searching for something.

Then she remembered, and guilt swamped her.

'During the night, I heard weird noises. I should have checked! Ava, do you think Frankie's okay?'

Ava looked stricken. 'I don't know. I hope so. We need to find Miss Watson, and pray that Frankie's with her.' She backed out of the room, but not before Samia heard her say, in a strangled whisper. 'If anything has happened to him, I'll never forgive myself.'

WHERE ARE WE?

1. THE HEADQUARTERS OF THE EUROPEAN UNION IS IN THIS SMALL COUNTRY.

2. NEARLY ALL OF THIS COUNTRY'S POPULATION LIVE IN CITIES.

3. ITS NATIONAL FLAG HAS THE SAME THREE COLOURS AS THE GERMAN FLAG.

17

A BOWMAN IN BRUSSELS

Samia raced, heart pounding, to the adjoining carriage door. When she peered through the glass she could see Miss Watson sitting alone, sipping an Earl Grey tea and staring pensively at her reflection in the train window. Doubling back before she was spotted, Samia crashed into Ava.

'Frankie's not there. Miss Watson's by herself, having breakfast. Ava, do you think he's been kidnapped?'

Ava's eyes were round as a barn owl's, her face ghost-pale. 'Oh, no. Oh, no. This is all my fault,' she whispered. 'What if he was dragged off the train when it stopped during the night? What if he's somewhere in Germany? How will we ever find him?'

Samia shook her head. 'Stop it, Ava. Don't be so daft. How can this possibly be your fault? Stop stressing, so we can think clearly. I heard the weird noises AFTER the train left Munich. So, I reckon he's still somewhere on the Métro.'

She tried to push away the memory of the man being shot on the train to Paris. The thought that harm might have come to Frankie was unbearable. They'd only known each other a short time, but he felt like a true friend. She loved his cheeky grin, his daft jokes, his kind heart.

'Let's check the unoccupied cabins, the toilets, the storage areas. If he's on this train, we'll find him.'

But hunting for a missing person on the Euro Métro was easier said than done. The storage areas and kitchen were all inaccessible to passengers. And they disturbed the dark-haired Italian lady, who shrieked like a parrot and slammed her cabin door in their faces, when they pushed it ajar, thinking the room was empty.

The only clue was in one of the toilets, where all the paper towels had been pulled out of the dispenser and strewn on the floor, but neither girl could work out the significance of that.

'It's no good, Samia. We'll have to go and tell Miss Watson that something terrible has happened to Frankie.'

Samia's feet felt heavy as lead weights, as the carriage door slid open and she dragged herself towards Miss Watson's table. She'd almost reached it, when she realised she'd made a stupid, stupid mistake.

Frankie had been at the table all the time, slumped on the bench opposite Miss Watson, his head curled almost to his chest.

Releasing the breath she'd been holding, Samia flung herself down beside him. She clutched the tabletop, trying to steady herself, and to rid her brain of all the terrible scenarios she'd been imagining. It was hard to feel relief though, when Frankie lifted his head. He looked dreadful: grey-faced, his eyes red-rimmed as if he'd been crying.

Something awful HAS happened.

'Frankie?' Ava's voice wobbled. 'Hey, pal, are you okay?'

Miss Watson, impeccably dressed in a dove-grey skirt and candy-pink striped blouse, poured herself more tea from the pot. Her mouth was tight, unsmiling. 'Francis has spent a very uncomfortable, sleepless night. Unfortunately, he broke a cardinal rule. He made the decision to leave his cabin during the night, and stupidly, he left the door open.'

'I needed to pee,' muttered Frankie, and fell silent because the waitress had arrived at their table. It was only when the woman placed a small tray in front of her, holding a glass of fresh orange juice, two buttery croissants and a little pot of raspberry jam, that Samia realised she was starving.

As she spread jam on flaky pastry, Frankie continued his explanation.

'I was on my way back, after I'd been to the cludge, when I heard a noise inside my cabin. Sounded like aw my things were bein hurled on the flair. I pushed the door a wee bit an I could see my stuff, flyin aroon. My boxers, an aw.'

He shivered, and Samia could imagine his fear and panic, standing outside his room in the dead of night, wondering what on earth to do.

After taking a large swig of juice, Frankie carried on talking.

'I thought aboot chappin Miss Watson's door, but was scared Marlena would hear me. So I went back to the wee cludge, locked myself in, an waited.'

'You spent the night in the toilet?' gasped Ava.

'Aye. It wasn't wan bit comfy. An now I'm puggled.'

The significance of the strewn paper towels suddenly became clear. Poor Frankie had tried to use them as his pillow and mattress last night.

Miss Watson took a last sip of tea and placed her cup in the saucer. 'Well, apart from the fact you'll be too tired to make the most of your day, no harm has been done. When the girls have finished breakfast, perhaps they'd be kind enough to assist in helping to set the cabin to rights?'

Samia spluttered, croissant crumbs flying everywhere. 'No harm done? Look at the state of wee Frankie! He's shaking!'

'I'm brand new,' growled Frankie, a flush staining his pale cheeks.

'I'm really glad you didn't go back into the room, Frankie.' Samia sharpened her tone, aiming the barb at Miss Watson. 'Marlena would probably have killed you.'

'He's okay, Samia. He said so. No harm done.' Ava smiled at Frankie and gave him a thumbs up. She seemed keen to move on, almost giddy with relief, and it made Samia wonder again about her words earlier.

If anything has happened to him, I'll never forgive myself... Why on earth would Ava think Frankie's disappearance was her fault?

After breakfast, they went to help a reluctant Frankie to tidy up the room and make the beds.

'I can do it myself. I'm no a total numpty,' he grumbled, gathering up his underwear and socks and shoving them into his rucksack.

Samia picked up the pillow and stared at the dirty footprint in its centre.

'So, where do we think Marlena is now? Locked inside one of the cabins? Sitting in the other carriage wearing a brand-new disguise? Driving the freaking train?'

Ava laughed nervously. 'She's bound to follow us to the Tintin shop. I've no idea how we are going to escape with the target list with her sniffing around, waiting to snatch the memory stick out of our hands.'

'You make her sound like my Auntie Mariam's Labrador when there's food about. Marlena's more like a cobra, curled in a basket, ready to strike.' Samia sighed and straightened the duvet cover on Frankie's bunk. 'I wish Miss Watson would just admit that we're in deadly danger.'

'And would me saying it aloud make you feel better?'

At the sound of Miss Watson's crisp voice, they all jumped. There was no room for another person in the tiny cabin, so she remained at the door, and continued to speak, in the same sharp tone. 'Would an admission your lives may be in danger do anything to improve our situation?'

Samia opened her mouth to respond, but Miss Watson answered her own question. 'No, it would not. But you are right, Samia. This situation is becoming increasingly dangerous and Marlena Malcoeur is becoming more desperate. She will have spent months, if not years, planning her latest atrocity, and the last thing she will want is for her plans to end up in the hands of MI6.' She nodded, mouth firm, as if she'd come to a decision. 'The best course of action is for me to book a hotel room for you three today. You can relax together and watch some television. I will go to the Tintin shop alone and complete this mission.'

Ava shook her head, eyes blazing. 'No way! We got all the clues. We got you this far. You couldn't have done this without us. And now you want to step in and take all the glory? That's not happening. We're coming too... aren't we guys?'

'Too right. I'm no goin hame til that bampot's in the jail, just for slingin my kecks aw ower the flair.'

Samia nodded, a bit lamely. It was all getting rather

alarming, and she wasn't sure she had the courage to face an "increasingly dangerous situation" with a "desperate" villain. The only thing she was absolutely certain about was that she didn't want to be left behind. If Ava and Frankie were going with Miss Watson, so was she.

So, leaving their luggage behind in Brussels Central Station, they walked out into a cloudy grey morning. To begin their whistle-stop tour, Miss Watson led them to a bronze statue of a small boy peeing in a fountain.

Giggling, Ava nudged Frankie. 'Oi, look at that guy! Remind you of anyone?'

Frankie who still looked pale and tired, managed a ghost of his cheeky grin. 'Least I went to the cludge. I didn't wee in the toon square.'

Miss Watson managed to maintain a straight face, but her eyes twinkled as she tried to remonstrate with them.

'Children, please stop sniggering. Urination is a natural bodily function. This little bronze is known as the *Manneken Pis*, and he is a much-loved Brussels landmark. He has an outfit for almost every occasion in the city's calendar. Unfortunately, he isn't wearing one of them today.'

She sighed, because all three children were now doubled up with laughter. 'Now, let us move on.'

Brussel's Grand Place was only a five-minute walk and was as splendid as its name. Miss Watson stopped in the middle and stretched out both arms.

'This incredible square is considered to be one of the most beautiful in the world.'

'It's not actually a square at all. It's a rectangle,' murmured Samia, but Miss Watson ignored her and carried on.

'Some of the city's best-known chocolatiers still have their shops in the arcades here.'

'Finally, some interesting info.' Ava grinned cheekily and swerved into an arcade.

The displays in the windows of the many chocolate shops were mouth-watering: pralines, caramels, candied fruit peel, chocolate-dipped macarons. Somehow, Miss Watson managed to talk a shop assistant into handing out free samples, and the chocolate was delicious, but the price for even a small boxful made Samia backtrack on her original plan to buy some for her mum.

I don't think she'd thank me for spending that much on sweeties.

As they left the shop, it started to drizzle, and Miss Watson opened her umbrella.

'We mustn't linger. The Tintin shop is just round the corner and we have a mission to complete.'

La Boutique Tintin was on Rue de la Colline, just off the Grand Place. It was just before ten o'clock and the shop was open, but the entrance area was so interesting that they stood there for a moment, admiring the comic-strip styled windows, the large models of Tintin and

Snowy, and the black dragon on the tiled floor.

'That dragon appears in *The Blue Lotus*, the fifth comic book in the Adventures of Tintin,' explained Ava, opening the door and leading the way into the shop. In silence, she stood and looked around, and Samia noticed her wipe a tear from her eye. 'Uncle Griff loved this place. He was a HUGE Tintin fan.'

Miss Watson frowned. 'Perhaps if you'd shared that fact right at the start, we could have guessed the data we needed was in the shop and come straight here.'

There was a very long pause, and then Ava dropped a bombshell. 'I had a pretty good idea, to be honest. Uncle Griff talked about this place A LOT.'

A comic-strip inspired store seemed a good setting for Samia to become a cartoon character, both eyes twanging on stalks, bottom jaw clanging to the ground.

'WHAT? You knew?'

'Are you sayin we did aw that clue searching for nothin?' gasped Frankie, ignoring the group of Japanese tourists who were struggling to get past. 'That we could just have come straight here?

Without putting ourselves in dangerous situations. No wonder Ava was so upset when she thought something terrible had happened to Frankie.

They stood in strained silence, as Ava waited until the group of tourists filed past their huddled group, and then tried to explain herself.

'Uncle Griff came up with all these clues. He must have wanted them to be solved and I didn't want to let him down.' She scowled, her eyes fierce. 'And if Miss Watson hadn't brought me along on this trip, you lot would never have guessed the drawing was of Tintin, because, let's face it, Uncle Griff wasn't as good at drawing as he thought he was, so I got you here in the end, didn't I?'

Anger was etching grooves on Miss Watson's forehead. Afraid she might be about to ruin everything by saying something awful to Ava, Samia decided the best course was to try and smooth things over.

'Yes, you did. You got us here. And if we'd come straight to Brussels, we'd have missed out on the incredible trip around Europe that Frankie and I had been promised. We'd have missed a real adventure. It has all worked out for the best in the end.'

'True fact.' Yawning, Frankie rubbed at his tired eyes. ''Cept it's no the actual end, is it? We haven't found anything yet. Can we get a move on?'

Miss Watson appeared to be meditating. Oblivious to the browsing tourists, she stood with her eyes closed, taking deep, regular breaths.

'Give me one moment, Francis. These things cannot be rushed.'

Then she broke the huddle, and walked over to a display stand. Picking up a Captain Haddock keyring, she moved over to the counter, looking so elegant in her pencil skirt and matching jacket, that several customers turned to look.

'*Je voudrais ça, s'il vous plaît.*'

The girl at the counter smiled, took the keyring, and asked Miss Watson in perfect English if she'd like a bag.

'Of course! I really wanted The Bowman, but Captain Haddock will have to do.'

The girl looked a bit taken aback. 'I'm sorry,' she said. 'But I haven't heard of that character. Calum, do you know anything about The Bowman?'

A bearded young man popped up from behind the counter where he'd been crouched, unpacking boxes. He stared at Miss Watson, head cocked, as if he was judging her.

Then he ran a hand through his dark hair and smiled.

'A rare and precious item. Come with me, ma'am. I'll show you where to find it.'

As Miss Watson followed Calum into a back room, Samia and Frankie glanced at each other and shrugged.

'What the heck's that aboot?'

Ava took a big, gulping breath. She looked as if she was struggling to hold back tears. 'Uncle Griff's codename was *The Bowman*. It was top secret, but he told me, because he knows, he knew, that I can keep secrets. Fletcher's an old word for someone who makes arrows, you see. And a bowman fires arrows.' She stopped and chewed on her lip. 'That guy, Calum, must have been friends with Uncle Griff. Maybe, I could talk to him. He might know what happened to my uncle.'

But Miss Watson was already striding through the shop, her bag held firmly under one arm, Calum at her other side.

'Thank you very much for your assistance,' she said, as he opened the door for her. 'Come along, children. It's time to go.'

As soon as they were in the entrance area, Ava pounced. 'Did you get the info?'

'Hush child, of course I did. We shall head to the Embassy immediately and arrange for the memory stick to be sent to MI6.'

'I hope Marlena Malcoeur's no lurking, waiting to pounce,' grumbled Frankie, as they walked out into the grey Brussels morning.

Ava stopped walking, so suddenly that Samia nearly crashed into her. 'Do you think Marlena cornered my uncle at the Tintin shop? Do you think this is where he died?' she asked, a tiny tremor in her voice.

Miss Watson shook her head. 'Definitely not. Marlena clearly has no idea about the shop as a drop-off location, or she wouldn't be wasting time following us around Europe. My guess is that Griff made a quick stop in Brussels, dropped the memory stick with his friend in the shop and then travelled on to his next, and final, destination.'

'Bruges.' The voice was harsh, and eerily familiar. 'We caught up with him in Bruges.'

18

BEDLAM IN BRUSSELS

The speaker was hardly visible, tucked against a corner wall, at the edge of a dank, narrow alley running between the shops. But as the figure rose, Samia's breath caught in her throat. The long, straggly black hair and massive grey hoodie were no longer an effective disguise. Marlena was easy to recognise now.

Miss Watson wagged her finger at the three children. 'Stay right here. Do not move from this pavement.'

Fearless, she stepped into the alley, and faced Marlena.

'So, is this an admission of murder? You killed Griff Fletcher in Bruges?'

Clearly desperate to hear the reply, Ava ignored Miss Watson's instructions and edged forward into the alley. Frankie and Samia followed, although Samia's heart raced, and she felt sick with fear.

Marlena pulled back her hood, revealing the face from the photograph, thin-lipped, eyes sharp and cunning.

'Griff Fletcher? The traitor called himself by a different name. He said he supported our cause and persuaded us to let him join our group. We trusted him, and he betrayed us. In Bruges we asked him nicely to tell us the whereabouts of the data he'd stolen . But he refused and tried to make his escape. His treacherous behaviour left us with no choice but to take him out in a small boat and let him take his chances in the water.'

Ava wailed, a terrible, heart-breaking sound. 'You evil witch…'

She tried to push past Miss Watson, who stood her ground and gripped Ava's arm. 'Stay back, child, for heaven's sake. Do not get involved. Remember she is armed.'

Moving closer, ignoring the danger she had just warned Ava about, Miss Watson glared at Marlena. 'You will pay for murdering an innocent man, Marlena. And don't try to deny who you are. We have seen through your ridiculous play acting. Your group is finished, all its members dead or in jail where they belong. You may as well give up.'

Marlena spat on the ground, close to Miss Watson's foot. 'Your so-called "innocent man" betrayed us. He stole from us, and he caused the death of my beloved brother.'

'Griff Fletcher was doing his job, to rid Europe of dangerous people like you. Now, let me get on with *my* job, which is to guide these schoolchildren around Brussels.'

'Liar. You are spies, like the traitor, and you are a pack

of thieves. Let me have my property back, and nobody else needs to get hurt.'

Miss Watson shook her head. 'I think not. MI6 are keen to view everything this memory stick holds.'

Without any warning, Marlena's hand shot out and grabbed a clump of Samia's hair.

Pain shot through the girl's scalp as she was dragged, twisting and struggling, towards Marlena. Within milliseconds, she was being held by the neck, in a grip so tight she was afraid she'd choke, so close to Marlena she could hear her harsh breathing.

'This ends now. I've got a knife, as the girl knows. And this knife has cut many throats.'

Samia stopped struggling. She stared into Frankie's eyes, which were round as moons, glassy with fear.

He looks really scared. This is very, very bad.

'Put your bag down on that manhole cover. I'll let the girl go, once the rest of you are back on the Rue de la Colline.'

Miss Watson took one step back, her hands tightening on the strap, her body language betraying her reluctance to part with her beloved handbag, and its precious contents.

Then, right in front of Samia's horrified eyes, the knife flashed, slashing the air. The girl's insides turned to water. Her heart crashed against her ribs. Blood pounded in her brain.

Am I going to die? Is she going to kill me?

'Do as I say,' Marlena hissed. 'Or the girl's life ends here, in this alley.'

As her lovely leather bag thudded onto the damp, dirty ground, Miss Watson visibly winced. With the toe of her shoe, she nudged the bag onto the manhole cover.

'Open the bag. Show me the memory stick is inside.'

Miss Watson leant down, unclasped the bag and rummaged in it. She pulled out a small, silver object and held it up. 'Let the child go.'

'Not until you get out of here. Drop the memory stick back in the bag, and then leave. Hurry.'

Marlena sliced the air again, the knife blade perilously close to Samia's cheek. Outwardly cool, Miss Watson did as she was ordered and began backing away, gesturing at Ava and Frankie to do the same. For a moment, the two children remained stiff and still, as if they'd been turned to stone like the trolls in the Hobbit, until Miss Watson tugged at their sleeves and pulled them backwards, towards the Rue de la Colline.

As soon as Miss Watson stepped onto the main road, Marlena let Samia go, shoving her so hard she tumbled onto the alley's litter-strewn cobbles. As she staggered to her feet, Marlena snatched up Miss Watson's bag and ran, clattering down the alley in her clumpy boots, making her escape.

Breathing hard, blinded by tears, Samia became

aware of more running footsteps, as Ava and Frankie dashed towards her.

'Are you awright? You're no hurt?'

While Frankie wiped the dirt from Samia's knees, and told her how brave she'd been, and how great it was that she was okay, and that nothing else mattered, Ava swore like a drunk football fan, and swung her fists at the empty air, anger and grief burning in her eyes.

'I'm okay, Frankie,' murmured Samia. 'I think maybe Ava's the one who needs help here.'

Proving the point, Ava suddenly collapsed against the wall, her entire body shaking with sobs.

'My uncle's dead. He's definitely dead. They left him to drown,' she wept. 'And, after all the trouble we went to, following all these crazy clues, after everything Uncle Griff suffered, that evil cow has just snatched it out of our hands.'

Frankie rubbed at his eyes. He looked exhausted. 'From the flair, no our hauns, to be strictly accurate, but aye, I'm scunnered too. It's no fair.'

Miss Watson was standing a little apart, twirling her umbrella, as if they were all making a fuss about nothing, and she was waiting for them to realise that and calm down.

'I think we ought to visit one of Brussel's many gauferies and have hot chocolates with Belgian waffles. Does that not sound a lovely idea?'

Eyes blinking in disbelief, Samia looked at Miss Watson.

'Are you for real? I've just had a knife held against my throat. I've almost been scalped and I'm pretty sure my knees are bleeding. Ava's beside herself because she's just had confirmation that Griff's dead. Marlena has just snatched the memory stick we've gone to so much trouble to find. Frankie's shattered after last night's terrifying experience. I REALLY don't think hot chocolate's going to fix all that.'

Miss Watson seemed completely unperturbed by Samia's outburst. 'No, it will not fix what has happened. But it will make you all feel a little better, and I heartily wish for that.' She smiled. 'Also, I have a small piece of good news to share. Marlena may think she has won, but she has done nothing of the kind.'

Unbuttoning her grey jacket, she revealed a large internal pocket. 'Passports, tickets, money and a very important memory stick, which I am about to drop off at the Embassy for the attention of my colleagues in MI6. We have completed our mission, children. It is over. We can spend the rest of our trip solely on enjoying cultural pursuits. An afternoon in Bruges, perhaps, and then a final day in London tomorrow?'

It is over.

A few moments ago, trapped in a dank alley, held round the neck by a knife-wielding maniac, she'd have been delighted by the prospect of this adventure being over. But now, with Marlena scuttling like a spider back to her hide-out, gloating about her victory, Samia didn't want their trip to be over. Despite what had just happened, she really wanted to stay in Europe for a little longer, enjoying Frankie and Ava's company and all the wonderful sights. And she really, *really* wanted Marlena to be thrown in jail.

She gave her filthy knees a final rub. They hurt, but not *that* badly.

'On second thoughts, Miss Watson, hot chocolate and sugary waffles sound fab.'

Brushing away tears, Ava gave a watery smile. 'Yeah, okay, if Sam's up for it. And sugar's good for shock. But I want my waffles with strawberries and chocolate sauce.'

'Do the waffles come wi maple syrup? I don't think I had enough o that at breakfast.'

They all had waffles, even Miss Watson. It was hard to choose one topping, so Samia ordered hers with caramelised banana, vanilla ice cream and maple syrup, since she'd had a *serious* shock, and liked the sound of Ava's cure.

After Miss Watson had made a quick detour to the British Embassy, to drop off the memory stick, they took a train to Bruges, which was less than 90 minutes away from Brussels. Bruges turned out to be delightful, with cobbled lanes, canal bridges and a main square of multicoloured buildings that looked like the setting of a children's picture book. As they walked along the sides of the canals, watching the ducks diving for food and a pair of majestic swans gliding through the water, Samia glanced at Ava and noticed the sadness in her eyes.

'Are you thinking about your Uncle Griff?' she whispered. 'I reckon he'd be so, so proud of you.'

'Thanks, Sam. I hope you're right. We did it, didn't we? And now the grown-ups get to take over.' She sighed. 'I *so* wanted to see Marlena getting arrested.'

Miss Watson, who seemed to have x-ray hearing, spoke up. 'Focus on the positive, my dear. MI6 are on Marlena's tail. Her plans are no longer secret. And she has no idea that the memory stick in my handbag holds nothing of any interest to her. Hopefully, she will be in such a rush to destroy it that she won't even check, and will fall into a trap we have helped to set.'

'Yeah, maybe. But I'd have liked to *see* her fall.'

In the afternoon, they climbed the many steps to the top of the medieval bell tower and enjoyed the views from the top, ate fries with mayonnaise for lunch, and, probably because Frankie was white-faced with exhaustion, went on a leisurely canal boat ride.

On the return train journey, he fell asleep right away, head lolling against the glass. When Ava nodded off, Samia thought she'd better pretend to sleep too, rather than endure strained small talk with Miss Watson.

When the conductor stopped to check their tickets, Samia was still wide awake, despite her eyes being tightly closed.

'Good afternoon, ma'am.' The man spoke English, in a clipped formal voice. 'I trust you are enjoying our beautiful country.'

There was a short silence before Miss Watson answered. '*It is chillier in the north than it is in the south.*'

Intrigued by this bizarre reply, Samia opened one eye, and saw the conductor passing an envelope to Miss Watson before walking off. Miss Watson opened the envelope, pulled out a letter and began to read.

Curiosity got the better of Samia. 'Was that some kind of code you two were using? What does the letter say?'

'My goodness, child. Curiosity killed the cat, so it's as well you're not a feline. Firstly, yes it was a code and secondly, this letter says that Interpol would like my assistance. Our experts have established that Marlena Malcoeur's plan is to destroy an artwork in the Rijks Museum in Amsterdam. Our friends at Interpol have been informed that Marlena is a master of disguise and they would like me to go to the museum tomorrow afternoon and help them to identify her.'

Miss Watson's expression was serious, but there was a gleam in her eyes. 'I can't say I'm disappointed by this turn of events. It will be satisfying to see this particular mission through to its end. But I will completely understand if you want to stay away from the Rijks Museum tomorrow afternoon and I appreciate this has not been the culture-focused trip you were promised. I am truly sorry if you feel let down.'

For a moment, Samia gazed out of the window at the lush Belgian countryside. Then she turned to face Miss Watson. 'Are you kidding? Apart from a couple of very scary moments, this trip has been the best fun ever. And I can't think of a better way to end it than catching Marlena. Did they tell you which artwork she's planning to destroy?'

Miss Watson stole a quick glance at the letter. 'They are convinced it's Rembrandt's masterpiece, *The Night Watch*. But I believe that's just a calculated guess, based on the fact it's the museum's most famous work and the painting has been attacked a couple of times before. There are no definite clues, just two letters in the document's margin... *P* and *O*. But nobody has the faintest idea if they're significant.'

In a field bordered by plane trees, the sails of an old-fashioned windmill were turning slowly, but the cogs in Samia's brain seemed stuck fast.

P and O. I don't have a clue what that means either. But I think we need to find out.

WHERE ARE WE?

1. THE TALLEST PEOPLE IN THE WORLD LIVE IN THIS COUNTRY.

2. THIS COUNTRY IS THE BIGGEST FLOWER EXPORTER IN THE WORLD.

3. ALMOST ONE THIRD OF THIS COUNTRY IS BELOW SEA LEVEL.

18

AN AMBUSH IN AMSTERDAM

It wasn't until the train's horn blasted, signalling their arrival in Brussels Central Station, that Ava and Frankie stirred.

'Ava, can you figure out this password?' asked Miss Watson, as they hurried towards the Euro Métro escalator.

This one took a while. Ava slumped onto a bench and sat with her head in her hands, staring at the short string of letters, H W A R W E, while Miss Watson stood, tapping her foot impatiently. Suddenly, Ava laughed aloud, making them all jump.

'Got it! It's a Keyboard Cipher. At least they're making an effort now!'

While Miss Watson queued for tickets, Samia explained to the others about the change of plans.

Ava rubbed at her eyes, still tired. 'So, we have to identify Marlena, and point her out to Interpol?'

'I'm game,' yawned Frankie. 'If I get a decent sleep the night.'

Luckily, dinner was served early on the Euro Métro to

Amsterdam. Dessert was *appelflappen*, a delicious puff pastry apple turnover, flavoured with cinnamon and powdered with icing sugar. Frankie was highly amused by the name and used every opportunity to repeat it.

'My *appelflappen's* rerr. I'm goin to get the recipe for *appelflappen* an make wan for my maw. Miss Watson, would you like some mair *appelflappen*?'

That night, sleep came almost instantly, and Samia didn't wake until morning, when Frankie, all of his bounce back, banged on the door.

'Come on, guys, my stomach thinks my throat's cut.'

Ava opened the cabin door, and gave him a hard stare. 'Tactless thing to say to Sam, after yesterday's knife drama.'

But Samia was focussing on other stuff, like trying to find one more pair of clean socks in her rucksack, and musing on the fact that they had hardly any time left together.

We'll be heading home tonight. This time tomorrow, we'll be back in Glasgow. We need to make today count. And we CAN'T fail. We NEED to make sure Marlena's captured.

In the dining carriage, the waiter served stacks of Dutch pancakes for breakfast. Even Miss Watson smothered them in syrup.

'Are we stakin oot this Rijk's Museum aw day, then?' asked Frankie, spraying pancake crumbs across the table.

'Oh, no. In the morning, we are going to visit Anne Frank's House,' replied Miss Watson calmly. 'Followed by lunch, followed by our mission to the Rijk's Museum.'

Ava stabbed her pancake with a fork. 'Hopefully not followed by us being blue-lit to hospital with knife wounds.'

Miss Watson's eyebrows arched. 'We will NOT be involved in any confrontation. Our job is merely to point Marlena out to the police, if we are able.'

'Who bets it gets messy?' mouthed Ava, and both Frankie and Samia nodded in unison.

***

The visit to Anne Frank's House was a sobering experience.

As they walked through the secret doorway, hidden behind a movable bookcase, and stepped into the small annex where Anne and her family had hidden from the Nazis for more than two years, Ava had tears in her eyes, and even Frankie went silent when he saw the pencil marks on the wallpaper, made to track Anne and her sister's growth. Samia shuddered when she thought how afraid the family must have been when the soldiers thundered up these stairs and dragged them to a concentration camp, where Anne, her mother and sister died of typhus.

The cruelty and wickedness of the Holocaust was almost unfathomable, and the thought that some people still supported Nazi ideology made Samia feel sick with horror.

'After the war, Anne's father Otto, the family's only survivor, came back here, and was given Anne's diary, which had been found in the annex by one of the office workers.' Miss Watson explained. 'He had the entries published and Anne's diary has become one of the most famous books in the world.'

After they'd finished the tour of the house and the museum, they went for a half hour walk along Amsterdam's cobbled streets and canal banks to the Museum Quarter, where they ate a picnic lunch, sitting on the grass in the *Vondelpark*. In the distance, jazz music was being played in the bandstand. The paths were busy with cyclists and skateboarders. Samia bit into her *broodje*, a delicious sandwich filled with smoked chicken breast, crispy bacon and lettuce. She wished that they could stay here all afternoon, chatting and laughing and enjoying the sunshine and the park's lively atmosphere.

But we've got to face Marlena again.

It was as if Miss Watson had read her mind. She stood up, brushing crumbs from her lemon-yellow frock.

'Time to go. Don't forget, all that is required of you is that you keep your eyes peeled and report any sightings to me. Do not, I repeat—DO NOT—confront Marlena.'

The *Rijks Museum*—or State Museum in English—was located in a massive, cathedral-like building, and Miss Watson gave them a quick lecture before they entered.

'It is very grand, so do behave yourselves. No sniggering at the nudes.'

Samia scanned the queues of people waiting to buy tickets. How would they recognise Marlena, if she had opted for a new disguise? Left-handed people, and those with small moles, weren't easy to spot in a crowd.

A uniformed policeman appeared and spoke in an undertone to Miss Watson. He led them to a vaulted gallery, dominated by an enormous painting of snazzily dressed men on a dark background. The whole work was enclosed in a massive square glass chamber.

'This is Rembrandt's masterpiece, *The Night Watch*, the one Marlena may be planning to destroy.'

An officer beckoned to Miss Watson, and she started to walk away. 'Excuse me, children. I'll be back in five minutes. Stay here.'

Ava waited until Miss Watson had left before she spoke. 'I know I'm stating the obvious here, but this painting is in a massive glass box.'

Frankie nodded sagely. 'Aye, Marlena's no goin to find that yin easy to stab, is she?'

Samia shook her head, then looked round the room, at the security guards lining the walls, the police officer speaking to Miss Watson, the row of armed police

177

standing behind pillars.

'Maybe Marlena's original plan was to destroy this painting. But I reckon she's too smart to walk into a trap like this.' A thought dawned. 'I think she might have a Plan B, maybe something to do with the pencilled letters in the margin.'

Ava nodded. 'You could be right. While all these guys are standing around, guarding The Night Watch, she might have gone elsewhere to destroy some other famous artwork.'

'Which would make them look like a shower of dozy eejits,' added Frankie.

'Or maybe, she's somewhere else in this museum.' Samia was thinking aloud. 'That would appeal to her, wouldn't it? Destroying a precious artwork right under Interpol's noses and getting away with it.'

Frankie pulled a leaflet out his pocket and waved it. 'I got this leaflet at the door: *Ten Highlights of the Rijks Museum*. Let's check them aw oot. Come on.'

Slipping unnoticed out of the gallery, they began their search, made easier by the map on the back of the leaflet. First, they located Vermeer's beautiful painting *The Milkmaid*, but there was no sign of Marlena anywhere nearby.

'Should I stay here an keep an eye oot?' asked Frankie, but Ava shook her head.

'When the kids split up in horror movies it always

ends with one dying horribly. Let's not go there.'

The prospect of dying horribly wasn't at all appealing, so Samia stuck close to the others as they went looking for the next highlight. This one wasn't a painting, but a huge and elaborately decorated doll's house, spot-lit in a darkened space.

Frankie read aloud from his leaflet. 'Petronella Oortman was a rich woman in the Dutch Golden Age, who had a dollhouse built for her that she decorated with expensive miniatures. The house was a status symbol, which she used to show off her wealth... wait, this wummin was mega-rich. She could have had a Ferrari or a yacht, an she spent a fortune on a kid's toy?'

The doll's house was exquisite, furnished with miniature wicker and upholstered furniture, real marble flooring, tiny plates, embroidered cushions and detailed paintings on the wallpapered walls. As they gazed at it, Samia had a sudden thought.

'Petronella Oortman... the lady's initials were P O!'

Ava whistled. 'I'm guessing that isn't a coincidence. We should go and tell Miss Watson.'

Behind them, somebody coughed.

Samia turned, but couldn't see anyone, except a female security guard sitting on a plastic chair at the edge of the open doorway. As their eyes met, the security guard stood up. Face partly obscured by a peaked cap, she walked slowly towards them.

'This room is temporarily out of bounds. Leave immediately please.'

At the sound of that chilly, all-too-familiar voice, Ava and Frankie whirled round. Samia looked down from the raised wooden platform on which they were standing. It had given them a better view of the doll's house, but now it felt like a trap.

Making a guttural sound in the back of her throat, Marlena spat on the floor. 'So, it's you again. You children are certainly smarter than the stupid idiots huddling round *The Night Watch*. Did they really think I wouldn't alter my plans when my security had been so compromised?'

Bending, Marlena reached under a glass display case, and pulled out a large iron axe with a carved wooden handle. 'This magnificent medieval axe has been borrowed from the museum's extensive weapons collection. It is a lethal weapon, believe me. I suggest you leave now—unless you are willing to lose limbs.'

Samia noticed Frankie fumbling in his jacket pocket and remembered the fondue skewer he'd pocketed in Bern.

'Don't you dare,' she hissed. 'If you try and prod her with that, she'll chop your hand off. Let's get out of here. We need to get help.'

Shuffling sideways, eyes fixed on Marlena, Samia's feet touched the top step on the left of the platform.

Her muscles were tensed, ready to run.

And then Ava attacked.

Vaulting over the rail like a gymnast, she hurled herself onto Marlena's back. The woman gave a buzzard-like screech as Ava's fingernails clawed and tugged at her hair. As Marlena thrashed around, the peaked cap fell off and spun across the floor.

Trapped on the platform, Samia and Frankie cowered in terror, as Marlena raised the axe, again and again, aiming blindly for the doll's house. It kept crashing downwards, splintering the wooden platform, missing them by mere centimetres. Trying desperately to avoid the flailing weapon, Frankie flung himself sideways, tumbling down the stairs to the right.

'Go and get help!' Samia yelled, watching in horror as Marlena lurched to and fro, the axe swinging wildly, Ava clinging to her back like a baby monkey.

We're going to die. Marlena's going to kill us. This is crazy.

'Ava! Play dead!' The deep voice came from the doorway, loud and urgent, and Ava's reaction was immediate. Releasing her grip on Marlena, she dropped like a stone, and curled up on the floor.

As Marlena turned and raised the axe, panic surged through Samia and she screamed. 'Ava, get out of the—'

But she didn't finish, because without warning, Marlena crumpled to the ground. With an almighty crash, the iron axe smashed on to the tiles, missing Ava by millimetres. Cowering, Samia pressed her fists to the side of her head, unable to take in what was happening.

Is Marlena dead?

Behind her prone figure, a tall man stood, a satisfied smile on his handsome face. In one hand, he was holding a rectangular black object, and slowly, it dawned on Samia what had happened. Marlena had been tasered.

Samia tried to stand, but her muscles seemed to have liquified. She opened her mouth to call Ava, but no sound came out. She watched as the man turned and walked away.

The room was filling up with uniformed police and security guards, and Marlena was being dragged away. As the space emptied again, bar two uniformed officers, Samia saw that Ava was sitting up, hugging her knees, rocking, her eyes wide with shock.

Miss Watson's heels clicked on the tiles as she entered the room, Frankie by her side. Her eyebrows arched as she surveyed the chaos.

'Heavens. I explicitly recall telling you children to stay where you were. And not to confront Marlena.'

Samia clambered down from the damaged platform, her legs still wobbly, her heart thudding against her ribs. Walking over to Ava, she crouched down beside her.

'Ava, are you okay? You were so, so brave.'

Tears spilled down Ava's cheeks. 'I must be going

crazy. I thought I heard my uncle, telling me to play dead, like I used to do when we were pretending to be spies.'

Miss Watson gave a very long sigh. 'Ava, you did hear your uncle's voice. Griff Fletcher is alive and well. He was rescued half-dead from the Channel by a fishing boat and taken to a French hospital. Without papers, the medical staff were unable to identify him, and he was too poorly to tell them. He got in touch with MI6 this morning apparently, and couldn't resist getting involved at the end of this mission.'

As Miss Watson spoke, the light returned to Ava's eyes. 'He's not dead? My uncle's alive?'

Miss Watson smiled. 'Very much alive, and just as insufferably sure of himself. He has had to pop to St Thomas's Hospital for a thorough check-up, but has said we'll see him again soon.'

'I can't believe this. I thought he was dead, and he isn't. Sam, my uncle's ALIVE!' Ava sounded completely dazed, and Samia put an arm round her, and gave her a massive hug. 'It's the perfect happy ending.'

Bending, Miss Watson gave Ava an awkward pat on the head. 'Your uncle's enormously proud of you, Ava, as am I.' She smiled at Frankie and Samia. 'I am proud of you all. You three children have saved one of Europe's most precious treasures from destruction. You are all heroes and deserve a reward.'

Frankie scratched at his mosquito bite, eyes thoughtful. 'A Ferrari-type reward? Or a McDonald's?'

When she got on board the Euro Métro that evening, Samia's head was still whirling, trying to make sense of everything that had happened.

You are all heroes.

Oddly, Miss Watson's words filled her with more pride than if she'd been singled out for special praise. Ava had been incredibly brave, and if Frankie hadn't got help so quickly, they'd have been in dreadful trouble. In Samia's head, she could still see Marlena, cruel eyes glinting, clutching that terrible axe, heading towards that priceless antique doll's house, fully prepared to reduce it to splinters, and not caring who she hurt in the process.

When Miss Watson went to her cabin to "change into more comfortable shoes", Frankie held up his can of Coke. 'Here's to us. Best pals forever.'

As they clinked cans, Samia felt tears nipping her eyelids. 'Best pals forever,' she repeated.

'I can't believe this train's taking us all the way back to Glasgow.' Ava sounded choked. 'We'll be home in the morning. This adventure is over. I feel so happy, cos my uncle's alive after all, and I'll see him again soon, but I feel kind of sad at the same time, cos I'm really going to miss you guys.'

'Aye, me an aw,' Frankie took a large swig of Coke. 'I'll

be back at hame wi my maw, an it'll aw seem a bit… flat.'

Samia hated to hear them sound so down, and tried to lift their spirits. 'When we get our phones back, it'll be like the twenty-first century actually happened. We'll be able to chat whenever we like.'

Then she remembered something Miss Watson had said earlier.

'At dinner, on the canal cruise this evening, Miss Watson asked if we'd ever considered a career in spying. She made out it was a joke, but what if she was serious? What if she decides to take us with her on her next mission? After all, we were super useful to her, weren't we?'

'So, this adventure's over, but there might be another one coming soon?' Ava sat up straighter, brightening at the prospect.

Frankie grinned and raised his can again.

'To us… the Euro Spies.'

EPILOGUE

They'd agreed to meet under the clock in Central Station at three pm. Samia, anxious not to be late, arrived ten minutes early, and got twitchy with nerves as the hands on the clock ticked towards the hour. The last time she'd seen Frankie and Ava was when they'd hugged tearfully at the end of their spying adventure and vowed to stay friends forever. And they HAD stayed in touch, by phone, almost daily, but it was trickier to find a convenient time to meet up in person, when so much of each week was taken up by school, and after-school activities and family stuff. Three months had passed since they'd been collected by their parents at Central Station after the most exciting trip of their lives.

Samia's parents hadn't been keen on the idea of her taking the train into Glasgow on her own to meet friends they'd met so briefly. She'd wanted to snap that, actually, she, Ava and Frankie were going to be a whole lot safer by themselves in Glasgow than they'd been travelling across Europe in the company of a so-called responsible adult. But of course, she couldn't say any such thing.

They'd all been sworn to secrecy and were determined to keep silent, just in case they were ever called to go on another mission.

Mum and Dad had finally agreed that Samia could go, on condition that her sister Shanaz accompany her on the journey, there and back. Thankfully, Shanaz was happy to abandon her at the station and go and do her own thing. But the long minutes of waiting were making Samia edgy.

What if Ava and Frankie don't turn up? What if we don't get on as well as we did before, now we're not doing the spying stuff?

'Hey, Sam!'

Frankie was swaggering across the concourse towards her, his grin just as cheeky as she remembered. Her heart leapt, and she was so thrilled to see him her first instinct was to rush over and fling her arms round his neck. But she didn't, still determined to play it cool, until Ava hurtled between them and pulled them both into an untidy group hug. She looked so different from the girl they'd first met. Her eyes were bright, her cheeks flushed with happiness.

'Aw, I've missed you guys so much. Do you like the new colour? Every time I look in the mirror, my hair reminds me of our Euro Métro trip!'

They both agreed her new hair colour, shiny Euro Métro cobalt blue with silver highlights, was gorgeous, but Frankie was too hungry to be bothered with small talk and dragged them out of the station to the doughnut shop on Mitchell Street.

Squashed together, they sat on the wide stone steps of Glasgow's Museum of Modern Art, slurping Coke and eating their delicious doughnuts. The famous statue of the Duke of Wellington, complete with traffic cone headwear, towered over them.

'How are things at home, Frankie?' asked Ava. 'Are the carers making a big difference?'

Frankie who'd just taken a large bite of his doughnut, nodded, and wiped vanilla custard from his cheek. 'Mahoosive. They come three times a day, which is brilliant. I think my maw looks forward to their chat more than she lets on. An I've got loads mair free time. I've started after-school football on Thursdays now.'

'Aw, that's great, Frankie.' A chilly wind was whistling round the GOMA steps, but Samia felt warmed by the company of her friends. 'How's school, Ava?'

Ava screwed up her face. 'It's okay. Maths is good, English not so much. But Uncle Griff's coming up for a visit next weekend, so I'm looking forward to that. And I've got my pals to talk to on the phone, so school never feels as lonely as it did.'

Samia put her arm round Ava's shoulder and hugged her. 'I like chatting with you guys on the phone, but I miss being together properly. I'd love to meet up again soon.' Worried she sounded a bit desperate, she tried to make a joke of it. 'We could go to the cinema, see a spy movie, take notes for future missions.'

Pausing, Samia watched a scruffy pigeon peck at the scattered doughnut crumbs. The bird glanced up, fixed her with a beady eye. It seemed to be trying to tell her something.

These two are your best pals. Tell them how you feel.

She took a deep breath, and continued. 'Or any movie really, I don't mind. I just like spending time with you two. The spying stuff was fun, but...'

She didn't have to finish, because Frankie, who always seemed to know what to say, did it for her. 'Yeah, but now we can just be best pals, without being chased around by a knife-wielding maniac or being bossed about by Miss Watson.' His eyes lit up. 'Hey, there's a McDonald's roon the corner. Do you guys fancy chicken nuggets an chips?'

THe ENd

ACKNOWLEDGEMENTS

Enormous thanks to Anne Glennie at Cranachan Books, Best Small Press ever, for publishing this story and for being so enthusiastic about it, when it isn't even historical fiction and is only briefly set in Scotland. I am particularly grateful that although Anne pointed out the characters eat A LOT, she didn't edit out any of the café scenes.

Thank you all of the Cranachan authors for your funny gifs and supportive chat. I absolutely adore being part of Clan Cranachan.

Huge thanks to Sarah Broadley for being a superstar, and for helping to keep me and the rest of the Nearly Nanos afloat during some difficult times.

Thank you Angela Noble, Literacy and English Coordinator at North Ayrshire Council, for always being on the ball! Love that you were thinking about projects and curriculum links before the book was even published.

Thank you to all the European tour guides who enabled me to visit fabulous locations online while I was stuck at home during lockdown. You really were inspirational and this novel could not have been written without you.

Grateful thanks to some of my incredible local booksellers: Aileen, owner of the gorgeous Ginger Cat Bookshop in Kilmacolm, Sarah from the wonderful Book Nook in Stewarton, Gordon and Molly who run the beautiful Seahorse Bookstore in Ardrossan and Craig at Waterstones in Newton Mearns. You all make me feel so welcome when I visit and have been brilliant at organising events. Thank you so much!

And thank you forever to Ian, Sally, David, Matt and Emily for putting up with all my nonsense. xxx

Lindsay Littleson
March 2023

AUTHOR'S NOTES

Euro Spies was written when the country was in lockdown. To keep boredom at bay, I started booking virtual tours. For weeks, I visited various European capital cities in the company of tour guides, learning lots and enjoying the experience of virtual travel.

The idea formed that I could write a spy novel set in several capital cities in Europe.

While I love holidays abroad, and have visited many of the fabulous cities described in the novel, flying is always a bit of a trial. To save my characters from having to stand in endless boring queues, I decided to invent a means of travel that would eliminate barriers and inconvenience. So, Euro Spies begins at St Enoch Subway station in Glasgow, when the children step board the Euro Métro, which whizzes them to Paris and beyond.

I've always loved books with puzzles to solve and Euro Spies was definitely inspired by Dan Brown's The Da Vinci Code. Frankie, Ava and Samia are tasked with breaking some very tricky ciphers and solving some really fiendish clues. It felt more like planning a treasure hunt than writing a novel and I had an excellent time thinking up the wording of each clue and deciding exactly where in each city it should be left.

Euro Spies was such fun to write, but I wasn't sure what my publisher, Anne Glennie of Cranachan Books (Scotland's Small Press of the Year 2022!) would think. Luckily, Anne was really enthusiastic about the whole concept and encouraged me to add even more codes and clues, and to write *A Spy's Guide to Europe* to accompany the novel, which will enable readers to discover more about the European cities the characters are exploring and give them some help to solve the clues!

Lindsay Littleson
x

ABOUT THE AUTHOR

Lindsay Littleson lives with her partner Ian and their very noisy cat in Uplawmoor, a small village near Glasgow. Lindsay is an ex-primary teacher who now writes full-time, when she is not drinking tea and eating chocolate biscuits.

She began writing for children in 2014 and won the Kelpies Prize for her first children's novel *The Mixed-Up Summer of Lily McLean*. The sequel, *The Awkward Autumn of Lily McLean*, was published by Floris Books in 2017. *Guardians of the Wild Unicorns* came out in 2019 and was nominated for the 2020 CILIP Carnegie Medal. Her latest novel with Floris, *Secrets of the Last Merfolk*, came out in summer 2021. In 2015 her WW1 novel *Shell Hole* was shortlisted for the Dundee Great War Children's Book Prize. Lindsay's historical children's novels include *A Pattern of Secrets*, set in Victorian Paisley, and best-selling *The Titanic Detective Agency*. *The Rewilders* (2022) and *Euro Spies* (2023) are Lindsay's latest contemporary adventures for children both published by Cranachan.

Website: lindsaylittleson.co.uk
Twitter: @ljlittleson
Instagram: @lindsaylittleson